THE SECRET DIARY

OF

ADRIAN CAT

BY

STUART & LINDA MACFARLANE

©2007 Nartea Publishing
A Division of DNA Press, LLC

Library of Congress Cataloging-in-Publication Data
Macfarlane, Stuart. The secret diary of Adrian Cat / Stuart & Linda Macfarlane.
    — 1st ed. p. cm.
Summary: Adrian Cat recounts a year in his life from the ways to properly train his owners, and the friendships and bullies of theneighborhood, to his romance failures and successes.

ISBN 1-933255-23-4   (alk. paper)

[1. Cats—Fiction. 2. Friendship—Fiction. 3. Bullies—Fiction. 4. Diaries—Fiction.]   I. Macfarlane, Linda. II. Title.
    PZ7.M1666Se 2006
    [Fic]—dc22

        2006016850

DNA Press, LLC
P.O. BOX 572
Eagleville, PA 19408, USA
www.dnapress.com
editors@dnapress.com

Publisher: DNA Press, LLC
Art Direction: Alex Nartea
Cover art: Mark Stefanowicz (www.markstef.com)

Dedicated to all of Catkind
but especially to Brian and Amanda -
the coolest cats in town.

Special thanks to our cats, past and present,
Mistoffelees, Midnight, Macavity, and Mungojerrie
for all their dedicated research.

Thanks also to
Joseph and Emilie Conroy of
Stone Bench Associates Literary Agency
for all their support and help.

Table of Contents

1st January

(Feline New Year)

I am determined to become wiser, braver, and humbler. By the end of the year I will be idolized by everyone.

MY NEW YEAR RESOLUTIONS

1) *I will not be condescending to my humans.*
2) *I will not maul the vet.*
3) *I will only give my best friend Lucky really, really good advice.*
4) *I will not be afraid of Killer – the evil cat who rules the Lane.*
5) *I will be decisive – particularly about being in or out.*
6) *I will become the world's most famous cat.*
7) *I will not get fleas.*
8) *Most importantly: I will promote world peace between cats, dogs and mice.*

11:59 PM: I managed to keep every single one of my resolutions - all day! Though, to be honest, numbers one and five were extremely difficult. Humans and doors are so frustrating. Only another 364 days to go, so I'm confident I can keep all my resolutions.

Slept a meager 21 hours today – I think I might be suffering from insomnia.

2nd January

2:05 AM: Felt hungry. When I woke my humans they moaned and groaned pathetically. Eventually Trousers got out of bed and grudgingly served my food. Really! I expect a much better service than this! All I ask is that my humans love me half as much as I love myself - is that so unreasonable?

3:21 AM: Suddenly had the urge to go for a stroll. I had to meow *twelve times* before Skirt bothered to get up to open the door. Sometimes I think all the hours I've spent training my humans have been a complete waste of time.

3:27 AM: Changed my mind about the stroll – it was too cold outside. Pounded on the back door but got no response. I had to walk all the way round to the front and hammer on the bedroom window before I was let in.

3:40 AM: Jumped onto my bed and tried to rest. The most comfortable spot is on Trousers' tummy but every time I climbed up he rolled over. Couldn't get cozy on Skirt either. My bed just isn't big enough for three!

5:52 AM: Couldn't sleep properly so I got my humans up for an early breakfast.

6:10 AM: Wanted to play chase but Skirt and Trousers were slumped on the couch like comatose voles. Typical, they've had so much to eat and drink over the past few days they're incapable of carrying out their duties.

6:13 AM: Gave my humans the evil-eye to let them know what I think of them. In disgust I went to bed for a short rest.

9:00 PM: Woke feeling great. Sleep was a great invention.

9:01 PM: Struck resolution number one off my list. In future I will reward my humans with the respect they deserve - NONE

3rd January

11:00 AM: My young human, Brat, was playing with his silly remote control car again. I hate the way he plays "crashes" while I'm asleep on the floor. My body aches from the tip of my whiskers to the tip of my tail.

3:20 PM: I am in love! The most beautiful white Persian has just walked through my garden. Unfortunately my inconsiderate humans are out so all I could do was gawk passionately at her from my bedroom window. As she slinked through the hedge I'm sure she glanced back and smiled at me. As soon as I can get out I will search relentlessly until I find my soul mate.

4th January

No sign of my heartthrob, White-Beauty, today. I looked everywhere. Killer almost caught me as I sneaked along the Lane. He threatened to bite my ears off. There is something seriously wrong with that cat! He obviously hasn't made a resolution to promote world peace between cats, dogs and mice.

I'm so forlorn that even food doesn't interest me. I only ate to please my humans. I feel that if they go to all the trouble of opening the cans, the least I can do is eat the contents.

Spent the evening slipping off Skirt's lap. She's getting so fat there's hardly any room for me. I should have stopped her eating all those chocolates over the holidays.

5th January

I met my darling White-Beauty in the park this morning. Her real name is Snowball – such a pretty name. We went for a romantic walk along the canal and past the Sewage Works. She told me everything about herself; the naughty things she did as a kitten, the human family she has adopted and all her likes and dislikes. What she forgot to tell me is that she already has a boyfriend – Killer! When he spotted us on the canal bridge rubbing heads he was not amused. It took all day for my fur to dry out.

6th January
(Condescension Monday)

As it was Condescension Monday today I was particularly disdainful to my humans.

7th January

Have not seen Skirt all Day! This is strange for she loves cleaning my litter tray and right now it resembles a compost heap. I wonder if I was too hard on her yesterday.

I thought I'd found a flea on my tail but it turned out to be just a lump of dry mud. Nevertheless I spent hours checking for fur invaders. I am happy to report that I am a flea free zone. Don't know why, but I still feel itchy!

8th January

Lucky has a problem and needs my help. Again! His humans have brought a bird into the house, a parrot called Polly. This contravenes several of the 'Commandments for Humans' that date back to Ancient Egyptian times:

> *Thou shalt worship only Cats.*
> *Thou shalt not serve any animals except Cats.*
> *Thou shalt not bring any animal into a Cat's home -*
> *unless it is food for the Cat.*

Humans are so much less devout than they used to be. But Lucky hasn't trained his humans properly so he can't really complain too much when they do something stupid. Imagine the indignity of having to share a house with a bird! To make matters worse the parrot sits on its perch and repeatedly squawks, "Arrrrr, me hearties, who's a pretty little pussy?"

I told Lucky to take immediate action and advised him to knock over the perch, grab Polly by the beak and throw her out the window. That would teach the parrot and his humans a lesson!

(Personally I would have eaten the pesky thing but Lucky has had a strict moral upbringing and never kills any creature that can impersonate his humans.)

9th January

Discovered that the vet's blood is the same color as my humans'. Scored off resolution number two.

10th January

Spent the entire day thinking about how to become famous. After much deliberation and many naps, I decided to be a World Famous Mouse Trainer.

My Plan:

> *Catch mouse.*
> *Train it to do amazing tricks, like juggling balls and*
> *   jumping through fiery hoops.*
> *Remember not to eat the mouse.*
> *Become world famous.*

My plan will require oodles of dedicated work and will be difficult to fit into my hectic sleeping schedule. It's such a burden being an ambitious cat! I will put my plan into action first thing tomorrow morning.

My litter tray has still not been cleaned and I am reduced to doing my business in the garden like a common cat.

11th January

11:59 PM: Slept all day – will start being world famous tomorrow.

12th January

4:00 PM: Caught a mouse in the back garden. He didn't want to tour the world and become dead famous. He claimed he was quite happy living in an old boot in the garden shed. It was only when I threatened to eat him that he realized he did want to be famous. We started training with a daring stunt in which he puts his head in a lion's mouth. As there were no lions around I let him use my mouth. This was probably a bad idea. I got so excited about the stunt going well that I accidentally bit his head off. No great loss. He was so nervous he would have been a rotten juggler. Decided to become famous at something other than mouse training – mice are far too ungrateful.

10:20 PM: Tipped the contents of my litter tray all over the kitchen floor as a gentle hint to Trousers.

13th January

I went to see Lucky today. Took the long route avoiding the Lane for I feel attached to my ears and have no desire to lose them. Lucky's tail was all bandaged up! He told me that he got so angry at the parrot's taunts that he put my advice into action. He crept up and knocked her perch over as planned. But, when he tried to grab her, she jumped on his back and tore lumps off his tail. Poor Lucky had to go to the vet to get an anti-parrot-disease injection. Now Polly squawks, "Arrrrr, me hearties, who's a pretty stupid little pussy?"

Met Snowball on the way home. She wants me to win her heart by challenging Killer to a duel. Really, how barbaric. What century does she live in? Modern etiquette dictates that the way to woo a lady-cat is to present her with a love token such as a decapitated mouse or a comatose robin.

The contents of my tray still litter the kitchen floor. Trails of gooey white footprints cover the carpets. Come back Skirt, all is forgiven.

14th January

Skirt has been missing for seven days now! I have searched the garden, the alley, all the neighbors' gardens, the rubbish bins in the Lane (when Killer was not around), the park, the canal, the shops, the cellar, and the shed, but there is no sign of her. I'm worried that she's got lost. Humans are hopeless navigators due to their poor sense of smell. Trousers and Brat don't seem the slightest bit concerned. Humans can be so uncaring.

15th January

Good news! Skirt has been found!

This morning Wrinkly Skirt came round to look after Brat while Trousers went out searching for her. About time too!!

He arrived back in the afternoon looking triumphant. He had found Skirt, but she obviously hasn't eaten for days for she's as thin as an anorexic Siamese. And they brought home a human kitten – goodness knows where they found that. It is absolutely tiny - yet it makes the most unbearable noise and revolting smell. Despite the pong, everyone spent the rest of the day cuddling and hugging and drooling over it. It was sickening. They should only be cuddling and hugging and drooling over me. But they ignored me completely. In disgust I have retreated to my bedroom and will stay here until they learn to be less selfish.

16th January

It's appalling, everyone is still fussing over the smelly one. It looks like they're going to keep it. This is just not fair – I have not been consulted!

As I lay all alone and abandoned on my satin pillow, I tried to think of a name for the new baby. My favorites are:

> *Screecher*
> *Whiner*
> *Howler*
> *Wailer*
> *Shrieker*

It's obvious I will never sleep again.

17th January

8:05 AM: Woke up feeling itchy. I think the baby must have fleas and has given them to me.

6:20 PM: The humans were still selfishly drooling over their stray so I went to see Lucky. Lucky shared his breakfast with me. Then we headed out in search of adventure. About a mile from the shops we caught the unmistakable aroma of salmon. We hurried to the Uncanned-Fish-Shop and stared longingly into the window. The counter was piled high with the most magnificent freshly caught salmon. Normally I'm a fairly law abiding catizen but the sight and smell of those delicious fish drove me a little bit crazy - I knew I had to steal one. With Lucky watching from the doorway in utter disbelief, I crept inside and, with the prowess of a tiger, leapt onto the counter. Not being an experienced thief, I hadn't expected the fish to be covered in ice. I skidded across the counter knocking everything onto the floor. Jumping down, I grabbed a fish and bolted out the door. The fishmonger came charging after me. I suspect he might have caught me if he hadn't slipped on the ice. Fortunately Lucky broke his fall or he might have been badly injured. I dragged the fish into the bushes and waited for Lucky. When he finally arrived he complained that he was too sore to eat - so I had no option but to eat the huge salmon all by myself. Lucky was feeling dizzy (this seems to be an unfortunate side effect of being squashed by a fishmonger) and I had to help him to his house. It was fortunate that I did; his humans had just served his dinner and it would have been a shame for moderately good food to go to waste. While Lucky took a nap I scoffed it for him – well that's what friends are for.

11:40 PM: This evening I reflected on how badly my humans treat me – they have not fed me all day. I am starving to death! If I knew how to use the telephone I would call the Royal Society for the Prevention of Cruelty to Animals.

18th January

9:01 AM: Due to the noise, smell and continuing neglect I am forced to run away from home.

9:02 AM: I have decided to live in Acorn Avenue. It's a nice posh street and quite suitable for a cat of my superior breeding. Goodbye Number 42 Hazel Drive. To be honest, I don't know why I put up with rundown Hazel Drive for so long.

11:43 PM: I'm back home again, having failed to find suitable alternative accommodation!

My search began at number 2 Acorn Avenue. I discovered the back door had been left wide open. That seemed a good sign so I immediately decided to adopt this family. Excitedly I hurried inside to meet my new humans. There was no one to greet me; no welcoming committee, no fanfare – how inconsiderate! Undeterred, I helped myself to a huge bowl of Rabbit-by-Product-with-Ascorbic-Acid-Calcium-Carbonate-Potassium-Iodide-and-Cobalt-Carbonate-in-an-Authentic-Thiamine-and-Pyridoxine-Hydrochloride-Sauce then settled down, on a comfy armchair, and made myself at home. What a shock I got when I spotted Killer sleeping on the other chair. I made a very, very, very hasty (but quiet) retreat. Can you believe it - a delinquent cat like Killer living in Acorn Avenue?

Next I tried howling outside numbers 4 through 46 in the expectation of being welcomed in. There was obviously nobody at home in any of these houses for the doors remained firmly closed – except at number 38 where a sweet looking little old lady threw a bucket of water over me.

There was a Rottweiler at number 48 so I quickly skipped through gardens 50 to 94 with the beast in hot pursuit. Number 96, was answered by a human wearing a tight, black t-shirt with "Death to Cats" emblazed across the front. His bulging arms were completely covered in tattoos of snakes and lady humans. He is obviously a mass murderer. Although he shouted after me, "Come here cute little kitty," I didn't dare stop. I certainly wasn't volunteering to be his next victim.

I ran to my garden shed and hid, just in case the Rottweiler and the mass murderer were still searching for me. I crawled under my worry blanket and immediately fell asleep - I didn't realize running away was so tiring. I snoozed for the rest of the day then crept into my bedroom to continue hiding.

I am a fugitive, forced to go underground in my own bedroom.

I am now even angrier with my humans, for they don't care that I have run away.

19th January

Skirt woke me up with a big hug and kiss this morning. Then she fed me sweeties as I lay stretched out across my bed. For the rest of the morning I sat on her lap while the baby slept in his cot. When Trousers and Brat came home they fed me lunch and then we spent ages playing attack-and-kill-the-pretend-plastic-mouse. They have obviously realized the error of their ways and are trying to make up for their deplorable behavior. Being compassionate, I have decided to forgive them and grant them one last chance.

It occurred to me that, once it has grown a little and is properly trained, the baby will be an additional human to love me and tend to my needs. Having resolved not to leave home, I spent a long time thinking of an exciting, original name for him. I looked back at the list I had made but settled on the brilliant name Brat-2.

20th January

(On this day in 1977 Misty Malarky Ying Yang of the DemoCats Party became president of the USA and moved into the Whitehouse with her human Jimmy Carter)

This morning I commenced Brat's lessons in feline language. I started with the simple, but important, phrase "feed me." While pounding on the cupboard, where my food is stored, I repeated the words, "Meeeowh meehoww." For a human he learns quickly and after just six and a half minutes he took a packet of Mock-Mouse biscuits from the cupboard. However, he still has much to learn for he obviously thinks "Meeeowh meehoww" means "empty a packet of Mock-Mouse biscuits over my head."

21st January

Wrinkly-Skirt visited. Every time I went near Brat-2 she chased me away. She must be worried that I will catch a sickness from him. (Old humans seen to have an overabundance of worry nerves.) But she needn't worry so much, I have built up an immunity to most humans.

22nd January

I am still pining for Snowball. Spent the day writing her a love poem.

Snowball you melt my heart.
Snowball, it is you I crave,
For you I would be strong, daring and brave,
For you I would climb the highest tree,
Or swim across the deep blue sea,
    (if I could swim)
To prove my love I would kill a thousand rats,
Throttle mice and slay vampire bats,
    (Note: not sure if you get these in Scotland)
To make you mine I would do anything,
Just don't ask me to fight that evil brute Killer.
    (sorry, couldn't find a word that rhymed)

The next time I meet Snowball I will win her affection by reciting my poem. (I find this option much preferable to dueling to the death.)

23rd January

0:01 AM – 9:00 AM: Slept on bed.

9:00 AM – 11:20 AM: Slept under television.

11:20 AM – 2:45 PM: Slept in underwear drawer.

2:45 PM – 7:10 PM: Slept in laundry basket

7:10 PM – 9:35 PM: Slept on favorite chair

9:35 PM – 9:36 PM: Slept on top of kitchen heater.

9:36 PM – 11:54 PM: Slept beside kitchen heater.

This has been an exhausting day. Deciding where to sleep can be very, very stressful.

24th January

Brat-2 pees everywhere! I think he's trying to take over my territory. I had to spend most of the day spraying all the furniture and carpets to reclaim my possessions.

25th January
(Catnip Day: 600 years since Catnip (Nepeta Cataria) was discovered in the deserts of North America.)

Yippeeee!!! It's Catnip Day!!! Raided the cupboard and ate a month's supply.

My invisible friend Contessa came to visit – haven't seen her for about a year. (It's odd, except for Contessa, I've never seen a pink, six-legged cat). We played chases around the living room and across the ceiling until I felt dizzy with exhaustion. Woke up after a long sleep and realized what a poor standard of tidiness my humans keep. The living room has overturned tables and broken vases scattered across the floor and the curtains have been torn from the rails. Humans are so messy.

26th January
(Annual Feline Day of Rest.)

Woke up at 6:00 AM with a dreadful headache. In fact I was sore all over – even my whiskers hurt. As today is a day of rest I went straight back to sleep.

I wonder why 'Annual Feline Day of Rest' is always the day after 'Catnip Day'?

27th January

Spent the afternoon helping Brat with a jigsaw puzzle. We began by scattering the pieces all over the room. At first Brat didn't know how to play the game, for he kept trying to put the pieces back on the table. Once the puzzle was completed, with bits spread over chairs, tables and floor, Brat howled with delight. Humans are so emotional.

28th January

While out for a stroll along the canal, I saw my darling Snowball. Round her neck she wore a purple ribbon with a tiny silver bell attached. As she walked the bell jingled and each little 'ting' tugged the cords of my heart. Oh, how I love her sweet and gentle charms. To the rhythmic drone of the sewage pumps I recited my love poem with great flair and passion. My romantic rhyme obviously touched her soul for she laughed uncontrollable for many minutes. However, she still insists that I fight Killer!

29th January

Can't write. Brat-2 hasn't stopped crying all day. I am suffering mental torment.

30th January

Brat played a new game this morning. It involved pulling my tail then giggling hysterically. I didn't like this game so I changed it to Scratch-the-Hand-that-Tries-to-Pull-Your-Tail. It's amazing how loudly a young human can yell at the sight of blood! After washing the blood from Brat's hands Skirt accidentally locked me in the cellar. It was hours later that she realized what had happened and rescued me.

31st January

Lucky came rushing round this morning to tell me that Killer has heard that I want to fight a duel to the death. (Who could possibly have told him that?) We are to meet at midday tomorrow at the park. I have not eaten or slept all day. I have however used my litter tray sixteen times.

1st February

7:00 AM: Stayed awake all night but not through choice. Scored off resolution number four, "I will not be afraid of killer – the evil cat who rules the Lane" – scored it out three times just to make the point. A thousand horrible questions tortured my mind. What will Killer do to me? How painful will it be? Can a cat lose all nine lives in one agonizing go? If Killer had been called Kittykins would he have grown up to be less aggressive?

7:30 AM: I am in hiding. If Killer finds me this will be the very last entry in my diary. If so I hope someone kind finds it and buries it with me.

6:00 PM: I am still alive! Yippeeeeeee!!! This is the most amazing day of my life – I was not savagely hacked to pieces by that paranoid, schizophrenic, egotistical, mega-cruel maniac.

Here's how I miraculously escaped certain death.

Early this morning I stole silently out of the house and crept to my ultra secret hiding place, the garden shed. I buried myself in my worry blanket and tried to blank out my mind. This may appear cowardly but appearing cowardly seemed a much better option than appearing dead. To my dismay, just before midday Lucky and Snowball turned up at my ultra secret hideaway to escort me to my death – it's good having friends in times of crises. Despite my protests, snarls, scratches and bites they eventually managed to shepherd me to the Lane to meet my fate. Killer had not yet arrived, so trembling I waited and waited and waited. Midday came and went but there was no sign of my evil executioner. Just as I was about to announce that I was late for another appointment and would have to go, Snowball exclaimed that Killer was too cowardly to fight and declared me champion. She said I was her hero and gave me a big smoochy kiss. As we began celebrating my historic victory, my friend, Mungo, arrived to tell us the news – Killer had been hit by a car. He was seriously injured and was in intensive care.

I was in such a good mood when I came home that I didn't even give

Skirt the evil-eye for calling me KittyCuddles. The first thing I did, after eating several tins of Faux-Mouse-with-Anchovies-in-Salt-Saturated-Brine, was to rewrite resolution four in big letters, " I AM NOT AFRAID OF KILLER – THE EVIL CAT WHO ONCE RULED THE LANE" – I hope being hit by a car is fatal!

2nd February

Spent the whole day at the Lane. For the first few hours I patrolled up and down to let everyone know that I am now in charge. Unfortunately the Lane was very quiet and I only saw two birds and a bee – but I left them in no doubt about who is king of the Lane. The next few hours I marched up and down some more – but with a lot less enthusiasm. Then, for the next ten hours, I slept – right in the middle of the Lane. I think that was really making a statement about who is boss cat.

Now that Killer is out of the way I can get down to seriously courting Snowball. I have never been so happy in all of my first life.

3rd February

9:00 AM: Got up early, very excited. I'm meeting my love, Snowball, this afternoon. Caught a mouse behind the shed – you would think that even the dumbest of mice would know better than to make his home in the garden where a boss cat lives. I will give the mouse to Snowball as an I-Love-You present. This will impress her and show her that I am a mean and powerful hunter-gatherer.

8:00 PM: Huh! When I presented the mouse to Snowball she squealed in horror and protested that she didn't eat mice. She screamed that she only eats Organic-Vegan-Low-Carbohydrate-Unsalted-Cat-Food-in-Bio-degradable-Packs. I had to let the silly beast go – what a waste of fast-food.

4th February

Today Skirt had visitors round for afternoon tea. I love teasing visitors! I like to sit quietly in the middle of the room and watch them. I can very quickly spot anyone who doesn't like cats. That's when the fun begins. Today my victim was a rather stout lady wearing a pink silk dress. Looking cute and innocent, I slowly edged towards her, purring loudly. "Oh look," said Skirt, "Fluffy-Kitty must have taken a liking to you." (I hate when she calls me that!) The poor victim didn't know what to say, especially when I jumped onto her lap. I showered her with affection, kisses and hairs. She particularly hated being licked on the lips so it's probably just as well that she didn't notice me spraying her pink suede shoes.

This evening I'm feeling rather poorly. I feel all itchy and I keep sneezing. I think I must be allergic to visitors.

5th February

Woke up feeling uncontrollably itchy - think one of those visitors has given me fleas. Spent the whole day grooming. Washed myself forty-two times but I can't stop scratching.

Despite my personal hygiene problem, I'm determined to become fit and strong. As new ruler of the Lane it is my duty to be far less puny than I am. I will spend all of tomorrow working out. By the end of the day I will have bulging muscles from paws to tail.

6th February

*(110 years since the invention of the mousetrap
made 300,000 mousers redundant.)*

Got off to an early start – woke my humans at 5:00 AM and demanded to get out. For a moment I thought that it was raining bird feathers - but it was only snow. Cold snow. By 5:04 AM I was back in my warm bed. Will start my get mega-fit campaign on a warmer day.

When Brat woke up he was all excited about the snow and desperate to go out. Straight after breakfast Trousers, Skirt and Brat were in the garden rolling the snow into big balls. I remained indoors watching from the warmth and comfort of the kitchen. They put the balls together to create a pretend person and stuck stones on it to make eyes, a nose and a mouth. It looked like fun so I decided to help them. Typical - they didn't appreciate my jumping on the snow person and they threw balls of snow at me. They thought this was amusing - but it wasn't - it made me freezing cold and icy wet! I went straight back indoors and will not speak to any of them for a week.

10:00 PM: Discovered that my pee makes snow melt so, to punish my humans, I've started to melt the snow person. I reckon than in another ninety-three days I will have destroyed it completely.

7th February

Visited Lucky today. Took the quick route along the Lane. It's great not having to dodge Killer any more.

Lucky was shivering and very upset. His humans had gone out and locked him on the wrong side of the door. Poor Lucky had been sitting on the snow all morning pining to get in. Silly thing, the answer was so simple, for the upstairs window had been left slightly ajar. I told Lucky all he had to do was climb up the fir tree, crawl along a branch and then leap onto the window ledge. I watched as slowly he scrambled up the tree, stopping occasionally for a rest – but being careful not to look down. (Lucky must be the only cat in the world who is scared of heights.) Eventually he was level with the window and began edging along a thin branch. The branch swayed under his weight but he clung on nervously and kept going. When he reached the end I shouted encouragingly, "You can do it! Jump! Jump!"

With eyes firmly closed, Lucky jumped. The cold weather must have affected his jump-bones for normally he could leap that distance easily. But he got nowhere near the ledge and fell to the ground like a sparrow that had forgotten how to fly. Fortunately he landed in a snow drift so wasn't badly hurt – I guess that's why he's called Lucky. Through tears, he asked if he could come to my house to heat up. Wish I had thought of that earlier.

Today my humans bought me a new chair. It's amazingly big, it looks fabulously soft and I expect it's wonderfully comfortable. I haven't had a chance to sit on it yet, for Trousers has been testing it out for me – all evening.

8th February

Spent the whole day meditating under a heater. Well, to be more precise, I meditated in between Brat-2's numerous screeching tantrums. Had an amazing thought - 'If mice were the size of dogs, catching just one would provide tasty snacks for a whole week.'

Trousers still won't let me climb onto my new chair - he's still running it in for me. How kind. Sometimes he's too kind for my own good.

Must see Snowball tomorrow - I expect she's missing me even more than I'm missing her.

9th February

Woke up with a pain that felt like hundreds of tiny teeth sinking into my neck. A vicious flea dragon was biting me. With a nimble left paw I grabbed the little fiend. As I was about to squash him into pulp he begged for mercy, telling me that his name was Kevin and that he was poverty stricken, starving and homeless. With tears dripping from his tiny eyes, he explained that, after he had become hooked on sniffing moth balls, his wife had ran off with his best friend. But now he was reformed, had joined Moth Balls Anonymous and was struggling to raise his family of one thousand and four baby fleas all on his own. In the past I would have been taken in by this sob story, but being the tough Ruler-of-the-Lane I can't afford to be sentimental. So I told him that he had just three days to get out of my house forever. I allowed him just one last suck of my blood.

Snowball was really glad to see me. I'm still her hero. But she spent most of our time together talking about Killer and how brave he has been since the accident. Apparently being hit by a car is not fatal. I wish I had started my get mega-fit campaign so that I could look ferocious and strong for Snowball. Then she would think only of me!

This evening I managed to get onto my new chair. Trousers thought that I didn't really want to sit on it and tried to push me off. I had to scratch his arm twice to convince him that I was happy where I was. But he mistakenly thought I wanted to spend the night outside in the snowy cold - it's just as well I've got a shed or I would have frozen to death.

10th February

7:45 AM: Someone stole the snowman during the night. All the snow has gone too.

8:00 PM: Spend the day relaxing on my new chair - it's purrfect!

9:00 PM: My humans arrived home with a present for me - they must have been feeling guilty for accidentally locking me out last night. But what a shock I got when they took it out of the bag. It was a yellow ribbon collar with a little silver bell. Skirt and Trousers both had to hold me down before they could tie it round my neck. Brat laughed and laughed and even Brat-2 had a fit of giggles. No matter how hard I try it won't come off. What an insult! What humiliation! What indignity! What am I going to do?

11th February

6:50 AM: I am a prisoner in my own home. Incarcerated by a yellow ribbon with a silver bell, destined to spend my life in gloomy solitude. I couldn't possibly be seen in public wearing a collar!

9:00 PM: Skirt was in tidy-up mode today and cleared out the refrigerator. As a result I had masses of sausages for breakfast, a huge haggis for lunch and freshly unfrozen fish for dinner. Overeating is very tiring, so I dragged by favorite silk cushion over to the heater and slept for ages.

11:57 PM: I tried again and again to remove the collar. But it's useless. It seems I must accept my fate and suffer this appalling misery.

12th February

I awoke feeling free and liberated. I felt unshackled, like a circus lion suddenly released from its cage and, for the first time, able to wander through the untamed jungle of its birth. I felt emancipated, like a bird freed from its cage, soaring high above a snow-capped mountain, swooping and diving in the fresh alpine zephyr. A miracle had happened - my yellow ribbon collar with the silver bell had fallen off during the night. Quickly I scooped it up in my mouth, climbed onto the window ledge and leapt to the garden below. I ran and ran for what seemed like hours, first through streets then parkland and into the woodland beyond. At last I stopped, breathless, under an ancient oak tree. I dropped my cruel manacle to the ground and covered it over with leaves. Never again will I be a slave to humans. Never again will I suffer the indignity of servitude. Suddenly I realized I hadn't had breakfast so I rushed home for a morning feast of Rabbit-Substitute-in-Oriental-Spicy-Gravy.

Snowball and I spent a wonderfully romantic evening together. Under the mystical light of the full moon we sat on top of the bins in the alley behind my house and purred sweet nothings into each other's ears. I think I am ready to settle down and have lots of kittens. Love is a wonderful invention.

13th February

Resumed Brat's training. As cat of the house it is my responsibility to ensure that he's properly educated in cat etiquette. Today's lesson was on personal hygiene. Brat had just finished a huge piece of cake and his mouth and cheeks were completely covered in chocolate and cream. I began the lesson with a demonstration - I licked my paws and carefully wiped the fur around my mouth. Brat giggled. I repeated the demonstration - Brat giggled even more loudly. I really don't think he takes his lessons seriously. Undaunted, I persevered, this time showing him how to wash face, neck and tail. He made absolutely no effort to clean himself. In the end I had to lick him clean myself, which was a lot of hard work but, admittedly, very tasty.

There is some confusion over my chair. Trousers thinks that he is allowed to sit on it. I gave him the evil-eye several times but he was too busy watching television to even notice. I will confront him about his impertinence very soon.

14th February
(St. Cuddles' Day - time for all cats to think about love.)

11:30 AM: It's Cuddles' Day and I've got a hot date with Snowball. To ensure I look and smell my best I spent a lot of time rolling about in the leaves in the garden. Being the romantic cat that I am, I dug up a snowdrop to give to my sweetheart.

10:00 PM: When I gave Snowball her present she ate it! Now that's a strange thing to do with a flower. Vegetarian cats have some very peculiar eating habits. Anyway she was delighted with the snack and we strolled carefree through the woods. We sat on Bluebell Hill and watched the sun go down over the Gasworks. Later I stole a haggis from the bins outside the Hairy Haggis Hospitable Hostelry and we dined together in the Lane (though Snowball didn't eat anything). What a perfect day.

15th February

Lucky came hurrying round this morning to tell me some devastating news. Killer has recovered from the car accident and is out and about again. I couldn't believe my ears and made Lucky go with me to the Lane to prove it. It's true, Killer was proudly parading up and down (with a limp) as if he had never been away.

Why is life so unfair? Why can't car accidents be more fatal?

16th February

Thought I should tell Snowball the awful news about Killer. But she had already found out. As I went down Beech Avenue towards her house, she was coming up the street towards me - shoulder to shoulder with Killer. I hid behind a bush and watched. As they went by I heard Snowball telling Killer that he is the most handsome, courageous, powerful and intelligent cat in the world. How dare she say that - I'm far more intelligent than Killer. Killer replied that she was the most beautiful cat he had ever seen - then they kissed!

Spent the rest of the day curled up in my worry blanket. I think I must be coming down with some awful sickness. I have a raging temperature and don't feel even the slightest bit hungry. I am diabolically miserable.

17th February

Lucky tried to cheer me up; "Love is like gorgonzola cheese," he said, "it smells and it's full of holes." It was no use, even Lucky's silly words of wisdom couldn't make me smile.

I didn't eat all day. My humans haven't even noticed that I am emotionally unstable and wasting away to nothing. Humans are so uncaring!

18th February

Spent today reflecting on what it means to be a cat and the conditions necessary for us to lead fulfilled and happy lives. I've created a list which I've called Adrian's Hierarchy of Needs.

For a healthy, contented life a cat's needs are:

> ***Physiological:*** *We must have lots and lots of sleep, more food than we could ever eat, plenty of sleep, loads of fresh cream and oodles and oodles of sleep.*
>
> ***Safety:*** *We need to live in a dog free environment. If all dogs were transported to Pluto the Earth would be a much happier place.*
>
> ***Love:*** *We must be worshiped by everyone - especially by Snowball.*

Esteem: *We have to be aloof and condescending at all times.*

Cognitive: *We must have the freedom to explore any and every box.*

Aesthetic: *We need to create works of art by scratching wallpaper.*

Self-actualization: *We need to excel at catching mice, voles, rats and multicolored-feather-things-with-a-string-attached.*

Transcendence: *We need to help our humans find self-fulfillment by showing them a little affection - occasionally.*

19th February

8:22 AM: Started today with a new outlook on life. I am completely over Snowball and feel better than ever (though in a forlorn and dejected sort of way). Decided to fulfill my New Year's Resolution of promoting world peace between cats, dogs and mice. This is my chance to make a long term contribution to catkind. If I can pull this off, cats will no longer need to live in fear of dogs.

11:30 AM: Full of enthusiasm I headed for the park to spread my message of goodwill. The first dog I bumped into was a huge Alsatian. Perhaps it would have been better if I hadn't bumped into him for, as he rubbed his bruised leg, he said some unrepeatable things about cats in general and about me in particular. Undaunted, I revealed my plan for cats and dogs to live in harmony. He didn't seem to understand for he began to snarl at me through flesh ripping teeth. Assuming he was just a bit stupid I repeated my plan slowly and loudly. Even that didn't work and before I could get out of the way his saliva foaming mouth was around my tail. Not exactly a sign of friendship!

With the most fearful hiss I could manage under these circumstances, I dug my claws into the mad beast's eyes making him release his grip. While the brute barked profanities, I made my escape. I ran until I was out of breath and collapsed on the grass. It took me an hour to recover my dignity.

2:55 PM: Realized that I had been too ambitious in starting my campaign with such a big dog. It would be better to start at ground level and work my way up. Carefully I selected my next convert, a tiny white Scottish Terrier. He looked so cute and friendly but I soon discovered that these dogs should really be called Scottish Terrorists!

6:04 PM: Postponed plans for world peace between cats and dogs but will try to create a treaty between cats and mice. I positioned myself at a suitable spot on the canal bank and lay stock-still. Within a few minutes a mouse came running up from the waters edge. I trapped her gently under a paw and told her not to be afraid - but she squeaked in panic. I began to explain my plan but she was so busy trying to escape she wouldn't listen. The foolish beast started gibbering on about some Geneva Convention nonsense. Hitting her on the head failed to get her attention. By now I was ready to give up - sadly it looks like there will never be world peace between cats, dogs and mice. This is such a pity for I felt an inner compassion for this wee, sleekit, cow'rin', tim'rous beastie. I felt that, although we were completely different species, we shared a common bond through the spirit of Mother Earth - kindred souls in the harsh struggle of life. But, being peckish, I ate her. With a glow of satisfaction, that I had at least tried to create world peace, I headed home.

9:50 PM: Tired and aching after a day of peacemaking I crossed out resolution number eight.

20th February

My humans went out for the day leaving me to guard the house. After a few hours sleep I was ready for the task ahead. I found a piece of string under a chair and spent the rest of the day chasing it - there is something magical about chasing string and I now feel peaceful and relaxed.

When my family arrived home Skirt and Trousers looked more unhappy than usual. They spent the next few hours tidying up the living room, gathering up torn papers, vacuuming, picking up bits of broken vases, mending ripped curtains and replacing tattered cushions onto chairs. They are exceptionally stressed, I should really teach them how to chase string.

21st February

When I looked out of the window this morning Snowball was sitting in the back garden. What a nerve! I decided to ignore her but, instead, rushed out of the house to see her. However, I walked up the garden slowly and coolly pretending I didn't realize she was there.

"Hello," she said in a quiet, sweet voice. "Where have you been for the last few days?"

I wanted to tell her that I was distraught with sadness. I wanted to tell her I was devastated that she had kissed and cuddled Killer. I wanted to tell her that I was broken hearted and all nine of my lives were ruined.

"I've been rather busy," I said sarcastically.

"Killer is well again," she said cryptically.

"Is he?" I replied, with an air of disinterest.

"Thought you should know so you can avoid him," she taunted.

"I'm not afraid of him," I lied.

"Would you like to go for a walk?" she asked surreptitiously.

"I have to look after my humans," I said contemptuously, wishing I had replied, "YES! YES! YES!" pleadingly, instead.

Moments later she had skipped through the hedge and out of my life.

Why are girls so complicated?

22nd February

It was a bitterly cold day. Lucky and I went for a walk and found the canal was wearing its winter coat of ice. The ice was very slippery so we played a game of slides. Lucky discovered that if he jumped from the bank he slid right across the canal and banged his nose on the bank at the other side. He discovered this eight times until his nose bled.

My feet have not thawed out yet and I can't stop sneezing.

23rd February

10:00 AM: My head is spinning and I can't stand up without falling over. My first life seems to be slipping away. I must have caught a deadly canal-disease yesterday.

11:45 AM: It's worse than I feared. My humans keep patting my head and talking in hushed voices. I heard Skirt say the unspeakable word, 'vet'. Normally I would run a mile at the mention of this cruel person but right now I'm far too ill.

1:30 PM: Trousers took me to the evil vet. He took one look at me and shook his head. I have heard lots of stories of cats being taken to the vet and never being seen again so, when he produced the needle-of-death, my whole life flashed in front of me. (It's strange, I always thought my life was more exciting than that.) As the vet approached all I could think was, "I wish I had spent more time eating cream." The needle entered my neck. I felt a horribly sharp pain. But I did not die. A few minutes later the vet gave Trousers something called 'The Bill'. Trousers seemed to be in more pain than I was.

24th February

7:00 AM: Too ill to get up. I'm lying on my silk pillow under the living room heater picking at a plate of tinned salmon and feeling miserable. Being sick is no fun, and it's keeping me back from my heavy schedule of naps and sleeps. (I always thought of salmon as being fish shaped - but strangely those in tins they are always round. I wonder if this is a result of genetic engineering.)

1:01 PM: For the past few hours I have been feeling really well. I have recovered from whatever fatal illness I caught at the canal. All morning Skirt and Brat have been fussing over me, bringing me cream and chocolates and faux-fish-biscuits. I only have to make a pretend sneezing noise and they give me a big cuddle. Think I'll be sick for the rest of the day!

11:00 PM: Have been stretched out comfortably on my new chair all evening. At long last, Trousers has accepted that it's mine and is sitting on an old hard chair.

25th February

Decided to be sick again today. While my humans pampered me I created this list of why it's better to be a cat than a human:

1) We are able to sleep twenty three hours a day and spend the other hour relaxing

2) A cat has twice as many legs as a human and, mathematically, an infinite number more tails.

3) We can see in the dark without the aid of electric light bulbs.

4) Cats can outstare humans and always win no-blinking competitions.

5) Cats have everything they want and have no need to invent

things like televisions, pollution and heart bypass operations.
6) Most importantly - cats can live without humans but a human can't be truly happy without the company of a cat.

11:00 PM: Overheard Trousers talking to Skirt in a hushed voice. He spoke of, 'vet bill,' 'economy drive,' and 'starting with that useless furbag's expensive food.' I wonder what that was all about.

26th February

This afternoon, when my humans returned from their hunting expedition to the supermarket, Skirt called me through for 'din dins.' There was a foul smell in the air, like a mouse that was three weeks past its eat-by-date. I snuggled up again in my new chair and politely ignored her. But Skirt persisted, "Come try your new treat," she pleaded. Reluctantly I made my way to the kitchen, taking a detour through my bedroom, the bathroom and the dining room. I discovered the source of the putrid smell. It was the so called 'din-dins.' In disgust I returned to my chair and remained there for the rest of the day. Twice I had to lash out at Trousers for attempting to sit beside me. When my humans went to bed I tried the Sham-Spam-Meat-Substitute-Ultra-Low-Budget-For-People-Who-Don't-Really-Like-Cats food that Skirt had put in my dish. It tasted worse than it smelt!
I have devised an action plan.

27th February

6:00 AM: Woke my humans up and demanded to be fed.
6:08 AM: Skirt opened another tin of Sham-Spam-Meat-Substitute-Ultra-Low-Budget-Rubbish-For-People-Who-Don't-Really-

Like-Cats food and put some in my dish.

6:10 AM: Stuffed my mouth with the vile concoction and headed for the dining room.

6:12 AM: Spat the 'food' out, making sure it went all over the new carpet and the wallpaper.

6:15 AM: Collapsed on the floor and pretended to be dead.

6:18-6:32 AM: Made choking noises as Skirt nursed me in her lap.

6:35-7:01 AM: Trousers went hunting in his car and returned with proper expensive food.

7:02-7:42 AM: Ate enough food to last a week!

10:00 PM: My performance today was so amazing I am seriously considering becoming an actor.

28th February

11:40 AM: When I awoke this morning I thought I was still asleep and in the middle of a nightmare! I could hear the awful racket of barking from just outside my window. I climbed onto the ledge to investigate. There was a huge van parked outside the house next door and humans were carrying lots of furniture into the house. A silly looking dog was running back and forward and, in between fits of chasing its own tail and howling at nothing in particular, it was attempting to help the humans. The humans gave him small objects and obediently he carried them into the house. Dogs are such pathetic creatures! Through fetching sticks, giving a paw and other such trickery they try to become man's best friend. They don't realize that humans prefer to be treated with disdain.

My humans soon gathered round the window to see what was going on. Brat irritatingly kept saying, "Nice doggy - nice doggy." I must teach him that the words nice and doggie must never be used in the same sentence.

11:24 PM: Trousers must have a short memory for I found him sitting on my chair again this evening. I jumped up but, no matter how hard I tried, I could not push him off. Eventually I had to share with him. I must put more effort into training my humans - I'm now suffering the consequences of neglecting my duties.

1st March

(Cat Nirvana Day - day of good fortune for all cats.)

My worst fears have been confirmed, a dog has taken up residence in the house next door. He's exceptionally ugly. I think he must have had an accident with a stretch-machine for he's very long and short. His legs barely keep his tubby little body off the ground. He looks really silly running around the garden barking at leaves. (His name is Brutus - which is very appropriate for he's a bit of a brute.) If I hadn't scored out my resolution to create world peace between cats and dogs I might have gone to the fence to talk to him. I certainly would have told him to bark more quietly for his noise is preventing me from getting my beauty sleep.

Brat-2 has not stopped producing those horrid smells. And he spends all day lying down doing nothing (apart from creating dreadful pongs and a lot of noise). Really! By his age a kitten would have learned to do useful things like chase leaves.

To get away from the noise of the dog and Brat-2, I went to the park with Lucky. For amusement we tried to catch a squirrel. These overgrown mice can really move fast and every time we chased one it would be at the top of a tree before you could say, "Six silly squirrels sitting in a circle." So we cleverly devised an infallible plan; Lucky would creep up from one side and I would creep up from the other. When we had it surrounded I would give the signal to charge. There's no way a squirrel could outmaneuver two nimble cats. We selected our victim carefully, a young thing that looked all tail and no brain. With all our feline cunning we circled our prey like two lions stalking a wildebeest. Silently, like eagles hovering over a rabbit, we moved in on the hapless creature. As we began to charge, the squirrel spotted us.

"Excuse me," he said aggressively, "can I see your squirrel hunting license."

"License!" I exclaimed, "What do you mean?"

"Don't you know that you need a license to hunt squirrel in the park," he said, "Are you completely brainless?"

Not wanting to appear stupid, I replied, "Of course I know - but remind me again."

"The law is quite clear," he said, shaking his head at us as if we were morons, "unless you have a special license, hunting is forbidden on bank holidays, full moons, Rogation Sunday, Shrove Tuesdays during leap years, the third Friday in alternate months, and of course on any day that has a Y in it."

"I know that," I said, my head spinning in confusion.

"So if you don't want me to perform a citizen's arrest," he said forcefully, "you'd better get out of here quickly."

As Lucky and I hurried away we could hear chuckling from the top of an oak tree. I think we were duped - I bet this is one of the days when a license isn't needed!

2nd March

Today I had an intellectual day - Snowball would be impressed (if we were speaking).

Wrote a poem entitled DesideCata. I am thinking of becoming a cat laureate!

DesideCata
Stroll placidly amid the noise and haste
and remember what peace there may be in a long tranquil nap.
As far as possible, without being in any way humble,
be on good terms with all creatures –
with the obvious exception of dogs.
Meow your desires loudly and clearly
and occasionally listen to others, even your human,
for she may be calling you for dinner.
Avoid the company of fleas,

they are vexations to both spirit and body.
Enjoy your achievements – particularly wallpaper lovingly
scratched and pieces of string thoroughly chased.
Keep interest in your career, there will always be a need for
good mousers in the changing fortunes of time.
Be yourself; especially do not feign affection –
except when you need a warm lap to sleep on.
Neither be cynical about the love of cream,
for through your charmed and enchanted existence it is as
perennial as the grass it comes from.
Take kindly the council of the years and rejoice in the fact that
you have nine lives.
Nurture arrogance of spirit to shield you from sudden misfor-
tune such as getting stuck up a tree.
But do not distress yourself with imaginings.
Many fears are born out of getting less than twenty hours sleep in a day.
Beyond a wholesome discipline be gentle with yourself and
groom yourself frequently.
You are a cat of the universe, so much greater than humans and
dogs; you have a right to be served. And even though you may
sleep through most of it, no doubt the universe is unfolding as it
should.
With all its snacks, adventures and peaceful dreams, it is truly a
beautiful world.
Be content.
Continue to be happy.

3rd March

After breakfast I went into the garden to find a nice spot to sleep. I was minding my own business just staring aimlessly through the fence into the neighbor's garden. Brutus was there, using all of his intelligence to chew the skeleton of an expired cow. After a while he noticed me staring at him and stopped chewing.

"Hello," he said slowly.

I ignored him completely.

"Let's be friends," he said with a grin. "Come and join me for a little bite." I remembered my resolution to promote peace between cats, dogs and mice. Perhaps not all dogs are evil. Maybe if I could make friends with just one it would be the first step in ending the Cat-Dog-Cold-War that has gone on for millennia! Like a mouse sniffing the cheese on a mouse-trap I accepted his offer. Through my friendly disposition, I almost became the first cat in outer space without the aid of a rocket.

The moment I stepped through the fence the horrid beast grabbed me by the tail. He swung me round and round and round until I was as dizzy as a hamster on a battery operated wheel with the on-off switch stuck in the on position. As the world blurred into a grey haze, he released his grip. Up, up, up I went heading straight towards the sun. Suddenly I stopped in mid sky. For a moment I thought I would be stuck there forever but I began falling - rapidly. Fortunately a tree broke my fall and I ended up dangling from its branches with the stupid mutt snarling at my heels. Luckily, when I fell from the tree, I ended up on my side of the fence or I would be shredded cat by now.

I have added a new resolution to my list, "I will get revenge on that stupid, evil, delinquent brute Brutus."

4th March

By chance, I met Snowball at the park today. I confronted her and asked why she had kissed and cuddled Killer. She insisted that they were just friends then asked me if I would like to be her special-friend. I asked her what Killer would think of that. She thought for a few moments, then replied that she expected Killer would rip me limb from limb in the most painful way imaginable.

So I have two options; being special-friends with Snowball and definitely being mauled by Killer or not being special-friends with Snowball and just probably being mauled by Killer. It's a tough decision!

Brat-2 said his first cat-word today. While eating a plate of gooey brown mess he distinctly said, "Purrrrrrrrr."

5th March

10:10 AM: I have decided that being Snowball's special-friend is just too dangerous. Instead of wasting my time on love I'm going to fulfill my resolution to become the world's most famous cat. I will be the first cat to climb Everest. I will begin training tomorrow, for today Trousers is out at work and I have the opportunity to sleep on my new chair without being disturbed.

10:45 AM: Brat has a new toy - a blue plastic whistle. When he blows it my whole body quivers, my hair stands on end, and I involuntarily jump three feet in the air. I am forced to give up my comfortable chair and seek refuge in my shed.

11:30 PM: My humans are all in bed. I am on my chair playing with *my* new toy - a blue plastic whistle. I have already managed to chew it into three pieces.

6th March
*(Anniversary of the Battle of Stirling Bridge -when
the Scottish-Fold cat army thrashed the invading English Poodles.)*

7:20 AM: Created my plan to be the first cat to climb Everest.

Today: Climb the poplar tree in the garden.

Tomorrow: Climb the biggest oak tree in the park.

Next day: Climb the huge hill beyond the woods.

Next, next day: Climb Everest - though if the journey takes more than a few hours I may need to postpone this to the next, next, next day.

11:20 PM: I began my ascent of the poplar at 7:30 AM precisely. I am obviously gifted with a natural talent for mountaineering for I reached the top in just four minutes. It appears that Everest would not be such a great challenge after all. The view from the top of the tree was exceptional - I could see right along the alley to the bins. There were two cats at the bins but from this height they looked just like mice. (Or they might have been mice that looked like cats looking like mice.) It was around 7:37 AM that the whole mountain climbing idea took a nose dive, for it became apparent that although I was an outstanding climber I was absolutely useless at unclimbing. In other words I was STUCK. For the first hour I acted like a cat who was enjoying the view from the top of a high tree. For the next hour I acted like a cat who was tolerating the view from the top of a very high tree. After that I acted like a cat who was terrified of the view from the top of an extremely high tree.

I meowed at the top of my voice, "Help! Help! Help!"

Brutus stopped chasing his tail and laughed so hard that he peed all down his legs. Lucky appeared from under the hedge and Brat stopped crashing toy cars and began to giggle. Even Brat-2, who was in his pram looked up and blew bubbles in amusement. It seemed the whole world had turned up to enjoy my embarrassment. But no one did anything to help. I meowed again and again and again. At last Skirt come out of the house - she would know what to do.

"Silly Pussy," she said, "come down at once."

Well that was as useful as telling a decapitated mouse to avoid dining at mouse traps! My fear and my embarrassment fought with each other to decide what to do next. My fear won and I continued meowing at the top of my voice. Trousers came out of the house and neighboring humans stared from windows.

"Addy up a tree," said Brat helpfully.

Trousers brought a stepladder and placed it by the tree. He climbed up but couldn't reach me. Just when it looked like I would be stuck forever a big red fire engine arrived and, as the whole universe looked on, I was unceremoniously rescued.

11:55 PM: I am curled up in my worry blanket while my dignity goes off on a long trip to purgatory. I am reconsidering my plans for I don't know if they have a fire engine large enough to get me down from Everest. I may content myself with being the first cat ever to climb the poplar tree in my garden.

7th March

Had a quiet morning recovering from my Everest exploits. Woke up to the fabulous bouquet of fresh salmon. Skirt was preparing lunch. I wrapped myself around her legs as a hint that I should get my share. She stopped making lunch and put a portion of Phony-Haggis-in-a-Venison-and-Wine-Soufflé into my bowl. It was time to turn on the charm. With eyes wide open I turned my purr to full volume and stared into her eyes. Extraordinarily, she managed to ignore this and serve lunch for everyone else. I patted Trousers on the leg to remind him that I love salmon. No response - except a playful, "Go away you greedy pest of a cat." No response either when I tried with Skirt and Brat. With the salmon disappearing fast, I had to resort to desperate measures. I jumped onto the table and took a great big lick of Trousers' salmon. This technique always works, for humans appear to know the rule, "Anything a cat licks becomes his possession." Minutes later the salmon was dumped into my bowl and Trousers had a salad.

8th March

A completely non eventful day. Trousers arrived home with his leg in plaster. His car was injured too.

9th March

All day Trousers sat on my chair reading newspapers and groaning. I felt sorry for him, so spent the day sleeping on his lap. I discovered that plaster is fun to scratch. Trousers thought so too and also scratched constantly.

10th March

8:10 AM: Trousers is using his plaster as an excuse to stay off work. I felt a duty to help him in this time of need. Had a brilliant idea! I will give him a present to cheer him up.

8:42 AM: Success! I returned from my hunting expedition with a semi-comatose blackbird. I left it on my chair so that Trousers could enjoy the final-kill.

9:06 AM: Trousers came into the living room. As he carefully lowered himself onto my chair the blackbird fluttered its wings. This startled Trousers and he fell to the floor where he groaned and moaned much more than a grown human with a leg in plaster who had fallen to the floor should have done.

9:12 AM: The blackbird, I took so much time choosing as a present for Trousers, was thrown discourteously out the door.

9:13 AM: I was thrown discourteously out the door.

Really! Humans can be so unappreciative!!

11th March

11:50 AM: It's like a madhouse this morning. Trousers is sitting on my chair (AGAIN!) grunting and groaning about his leg. Skirt is rushing about like a tornado, washing dishes and ironing and doing fifty other unnecessary things. Brat-2 is in his buggy, making smells and high pitched screeching noises. Brat is playing with a bow and arrow and using ME as a target. At times like this I wonder if I adopted the right family!

11:51 AM: I am in my shed hiding from my humans.

11:50 PM: This evening Lucky and I sat on the bins for hours watching the moon make its daily pilgrimage across the sky. Cat folklore says that the moon is made of green cheese and populated by mice that come in a huge variety of flavors. It's supposed to be cat utopia. To me this is a whimsical notion. I have calculated that if it was populated by mice the moon would have been completely devoured by the year 1742 A.D.

12th March

I was asleep under the rose bushes when I was awoken by that silly mutt Brutus barking.

"Want to hear a joke?" he yelped over the fence.

In the most arrogant way, I ignored him completely.

"Want to hear a joke?" he repeated in his annoying gruff voice.

"Tell me," I said curtly.

"How do you get a cat down from a tree?"

I didn't answer.

"Wait till autumn and it will float down on a leaf."

I walked away indignantly.

"Or call the fire brigade!" he shouted after me with a mocking laugh.

This is a nightmare, I can't even go into my own garden without being made fun of.

13th March

Spent all day resting on Brat's bed. I had a lot of time to think and I have decided that it's time to take control of my life. Over the next few days I'm going to:

a) Tackle Brutus.

b) Clear up my relationship with Snowball.

To cheer myself up, I made a list of reasons why cats are better than dogs:

* *Dogs must perform tricks if they want to be liked by humans. Cats are loved for their beauty, elegance, charm and pretentiousness.*
* *Dogs are unable to catch mice.*
* *Dogs have only one (very boring) life.*
* *Cats are free spirits and do whatever they please. Dogs only do what their humans tell them to do.*
* *If a cat falls he lands on his paws - if a dog falls he lands at the vets'.*
* *Cats bury their poo - dogs bury their food.*

* Cats have far more intelligent-thoughts in their tails than dogs have in their heads.

14th March
(Siamese Cat New Year.)

9:15 AM: Trousers must be bored not going to work - he has spent all morning tidying the living room and rearranging the furniture.

11:20 AM: I can't believe what my humans have done! They have stripped the wallpaper that I spent months carefully scratching into a fabulous art deco still-life. My life's artwork has been destroyed. Humans have no appreciation of the fine arts.

5:00 PM: Spent the afternoon down at the canal with Lucky. We played a balancing game on the bridge. The rules are - the first player stands on the narrow ledge for four minutes, the next player stands on three legs for three minutes and so on. Even though the ledge is very narrow, I had no problem standing for four minutes. Lucky did okay on three legs. Two legs was rather difficult and I struggled hard to keep my balance. I guess cats were not aerodynamically designed for standing on one leg - Lucky fell into the canal.

11:00 p.m. Lucky met Snowball this evening; he says she wants to meet me in the park first thing tomorrow. I have spent all evening preparing a speech. I will give her an ultimatum - she must give up Killer and devote herself to me or I will devote myself to unloving her.

My speech is romantic, passionate, persuasive yet forceful - with merely a hint of pleading.

15th March

7:01 AM: Arrived at the park.

11:22 AM: Snowball arrived at the park. Before I could enchant her with my speech she announced that she intended being special-friends with both Killer and me. As I stood, frantically trying to think of a witty reply, she kissed me on the cheek and ran off saying she would see me very soon.

Well at least I managed to clear up my relationship with her.

When I got home I discovered that the humans had put up new wallpaper in the living room. It's ghastly - not a single decorative scratch mark anywhere.

16th March

This morning, I watched Brutus, from the safety of the rosebushes. I noticed something that I hadn't noticed before - attached to his collar there's a rope which is tied to a pole. Although Brutus has freedom to roam across most of his garden there might be parts that he can't reach. I estimated the length of his rope and, using the simple mathematics formula:

$$Danger\ Zone = \frac{(Rope\ Length + Neck\ Length + Teeth\ Size) \times Velocity}{Desperation\ Index}$$

I deduced that he could not go further than the flower bed at the top of the garden. A plan for revenge began to churn in my mind. I crept silently through the bushes to the back of my garden, squeezed under the fence into Brutus' garden, then took up position at the far end of the flower bed.

"Brutus," I shouted, trying not to let my nerves show. "You have less brain than a lobotomized snail."

Brutus looked up. He seemed confused. I'm not sure whether this was due to surprise at seeing me in his garden or whether his small brain was trying to work out what a lobotomized snail is.

"And you have a very small tail!" (This is the very best way to insult a dog.)

Brutus assumed an attacking stance and barked as fiercely as a corgi can.

"And your mother was a mongrel."

This insult hit a sore point and Brutus charged up the garden at full corgi speed towards me. He was grinding his teeth in anger and foam dripped from his mouth. Behind him the rope took up its slack.

"Come and get me you good-for-nothing crossbreed," I taunted.

As his bloodthirsty mouth stretched out to slaughter me, the rope reached its limit. The collar suddenly tightened around his neck and took the full force of his furious charge. He crashed to the ground and lay in the flower bed amidst tulips and daffodils gasping for air. What a nerd!

"Good doggy, roll over and play dead," I sneered, "like the groveling little human slave you are."

Revenge is sweet.

Roaring with laughter, I skipped off to tell Lucky what I'd done.

17th March

8:10 AM: The new wallpaper is beginning to look more homely - Brat has been drawing on it and somehow lumps of Brat-2's food have been splattered across it.

While my humans were out I put a lot of artistic effort into adding asymmetrical patterns. Now, I'm glad to say, it looks just like the old paper.

9:22 PM: Rather than being proud of owning an art work on a par with Pussily Kandinsky, Trousers is having a temper tantrum. Nothing seems to make him happy.

18th March

Snowball turned up this morning and said we should do something romantic together. I suggested scavenging at the dump but she turned her nose up at this. After I had made ten other excellent suggestions she insisted that instead we take the long walk to the beach. When we got there we strolled along the edge of the water. Snowball said that the sound of the waves lapping upon the sands was like poetry and the sea wind blowing across the beach was like mermaids singing songs of love. To be honest, I was freezing cold and my paws were wet and sandy but I agreed with her. I added that the old rusting cans bobbing up and down on the waves were like, 'forlorn lovers, destined to drift separately for all eternity, like flotsam and jetsam on the harsh ocean of life, never having the chance to fulfill their dreams of happiness together' - but I don't think she understood the metaphor. (I expect this is because she has never experienced the sorrow of unrequited love in the way I have.)

We then left the wet sand and made ourselves comfortable in the long grass at the top of the beach and slept side by side for six blissful hours. (She even snores sensually.)

Snowball walked me home and we kissed on the doorstep. This has been a wonderful day.

19th March
(1st day of the mouse hunting season)

Today is the first day of the mouse hunting season. This lasts for three-hundred and sixty-five days. To celebrate this special occasion Lucky and I held a contest to see who could catch the most mice. It was a zero-zero draw.

20th March

It was a warm, sunny afternoon. I think the worst of winter is over. I hate cold weather!

Brat had a strawberry lollipop and we sat together in the garden sharing it - taking licks in turn. Strawberry tastes okay but to be honest I would have preferred a mouse flavored lollipop. I'm never quite happy about the hygiene of sharing food with a human - they bathe so infrequently.

21st March
(Day of remembrance of the time when cats were revered as gods.)

Today I observed my humans closely. They:

Fed me: 6 times.

Cleaned my litter tray: 3 times.

Opened the door for me: 16 times.

Fluffed up my pillows: 3 times.

Groomed my fur: 3 times.

Pulled my tail: 2 times.

Cuddled, patted and pampered me: 55 times.

Nothing has really changed since the Egyptians treated us as gods!

22nd March

After spending the day at Lucky's I was in a hurry to get home. Deciding to risk the shortcut through the Lane I looked carefully around for any sign of that beast Killer. The coast appeared to be clear but, just as I reached the end of the lane, Killer leapt down from a wall and almost landed on top of me.

"You puny little scumbag," he hissed cordially. "Do you think you can get away with stealing my girlfriend?"

"I . . I . . I don't know wh . . wh . . what you mean," I protested.

"So you deny your love for Snowball, you coward," he hissed.

"We are only special-friends," I whimpered.

"We shall fight to the death," he announced. "The winner gets Snowball."

"No need to fight," I assured him bravely. "You can have Snowball."

"Okay," he replied. "I will have Snowball . . . but we still fight to the death."

"Could we possibly do it tomorrow?" I said. "I really have a dreadful headache right now and I wouldn't like to die with a headache."

"Tomorrow? . . . Okay tomorrow at midday."

My greatest inspiration sometimes comes at the most unexpected of times. That's the odd thing about being a genius. This was one of those times. A brilliant plan for saving my life popped into my head.

"It's my right to decide where we fight," I bluffed.

"I'm happy to kill you anywhere," he sneered.

"Okay, let's fight in my garden," I said. "Be there by twelve."

I gave him the address and hurried off.

When I got home I stuck my head through the garden fence. "Hey, short legs," I yelled, "I'm going to pulverize you. Be in your garden at five past twelve tomorrow - if you dare!"

Brutus snarled an unintelligible reply which I assume was his dim-witted way of saying "Yes, my dear neighbor I would indeed like to rip your head off in a fight and will certainly meet you at the prescribed time".

23rd March

At 11:50 AM Lucky, Snowball, several friends, and about eight other cats I barely know (but who somehow sensed the imminent bloodbath) gathered with me under the bushes and jostled for the best views into my neighbor's garden.

At precisely midday Killer arrived and positioned himself in the middle of Brutus' lawn. Snowball tittered and almost got us discovered. A few minutes later the door of the house opened and Brutus came charging out like a bull who had been seriously insulted about the size of his horns. Before either Killer or Brutus had the chance to work out what was going on they were tearing at each other with teeth and claws. The fighting was fast and furious. There was snarling and hissing and yelping. As they spun round and round on the ground lumps of fur flew into the air. On our side of the fence, fourteen little faces pressed against the woodwork to see this amazing fight. We hadn't witnessed anything this exciting since Mohamed Ali-Cat knocked out Sunny Bright-Eyes Liston two years ago. By 12:20 PM it was over. Brutus and Killer lay on the grass - exhausted, aching, bleeding and duped. The fight was a draw but I was the winner.

24th March

Thought it best to keep a low profile today. Stayed in and played building blocks with Brat. He made towers, houses and cars and I knocked them down.

25th March
(National C.A.T. Day.)

Being C.A.T. Day it is my duty to undertake the annual adjustment of my humans to Cat Appreciation Time. Humans being crepuscular prefer to sleep during the night. This is extremely inconvenient as we are nocturnal. Annual training helps the human internal clock adjust to C.A.T.

This is my training timetable:

0:00 –2:30 AM:	*Played 'attack' with Trousers' toes.*
2:30 –2:32 AM:	*Demanded to get out.*
2:32 –2:40 AM:	*Stood in doorway deciding whether to bother going out.*
2:40 –2:53 AM:	*Went out - very, very slowly.*
2:55 –3:10 AM:	*Demanded to get in.*
3:25 –3:45 AM:	*Demanded to be fed – but didn't eat.*
4:00 –4:05 AM:	*Demanded to get out.*
4:12 –4:15 AM:	*Demanded to get in.*
4:30 –4:45 AM:	*Paced the room, moaning and crying as if in terrible pain. Stopped when Skirt mentioned the vet.*
5:00 –5:03 AM:	*Demanded to be fed – gulped my food down.*
5:04 –5:08 AM:	*Demanded to be fed again.*
5:12 –7:00 AM:	*Savaged the pillows, the duvet, Trousers and Skirt.*
7:01 AM -11:55 PM:	*Slept soundly in the knowledge that my duties are over for another year.*

26th March

Overnight Brat has had a horrendous flea attack. His whole body is covered in bright red bites and he can't stop scratching. Skirt looked worried and called in the Human-Vet. The vet checked Brat over and said it was a variety of flea called Chicken-Pox. Decided to keep out of the way so spent the day with Lucky. Polly had found a huge packet of nuts and had scoffed the lot. She was sick everywhere - in fact she was as sick as a parrot!

When I got home Trousers was curled up in my new chair, fast asleep. I jumped up and dug my claws into his legs but he barely noticed so I settled on his lap and slept too. But this unauthorized use of my chair needs to stop.

27th March

Snowball invited me round to her house to meet her humans. They seemed friendly and made a great fuss over me. They spoke to Snowball in squeaky hushed voices, saying things like, "So this is your little friend," and "Maybe we will be having little grandchildren kittens soon." Snowball made me taste her Organic-Vegan-Low-Carbohydrate-Salt-Free-Polyunsaturated-Cat-Food. It tasted like grass that had been pre-chewed by a flatulent cow but I told her it was delicious. Our relationship has become very serious and I think she may even stop being special-friends with Killer.

28th March

Went for a wander through neighboring gardens today. The door of number 66 Fir Drive was open so I went in to have a look around.

Everything looked so neat and tidy. My humans could learn a lot by visiting this house. I tested the bed. It was wonderfully soft and I nearly fell asleep. In the kitchen I met the human of the house, an ancient old lady who moves very slowly.

"Hello little puss," she said with a beaming smile. "Are you a poor little stray?"

Stray!! What a cheek! Suggesting that a healthy, intelligent, handsome, dignified cat like myself would ever be short of a good home! Before I could admonish her with a hiss and a scratch, she hobbled over to the refrigerator.

"You could do with a good feed to fatten you up," she mumbled.

She took out a salmon and sat it on the floor. As I tucked in to this unexpected feast she filled a bowl with fresh cream and insisted that I ate that too.

29th March

Having overeaten yesterday I had a long lie and didn't get up until 4 pm. Lucky arrived in a panic - a pair of magpies are making their nest in his garden. Magpies are the most viciously cruel birds in the world. They can make life unbearable for a cat. To have a pair in your garden is unthinkable. I promised Lucky that I would devise a plan to get rid of them.

Brat is still scratching at his Chicken-Pox flea bites - he looks so comical I nearly cough up fur balls every time I catch sight of him with his funny pink blobs.

30th March

Walked along the canal with Snowball this morning. She said that she will never be truly happy until Killer and I are friends. Girls have such strange ideas of what brings happiness. I felt like telling her that I would not be happy until Killer is squashed to pulp by a steam road roller, but, as we were kissing at that point, I thought it might spoil the moment. I have made her a promise that I will become Killer's best friend. This will be the most difficult challenge of my nine lives but I will do it even if it kills me!

This evening I was asleep on my new chair when I had a dream that I was flying through the air. I woke with a thud on the lawn and out of the corner of my eye saw Trousers slamming the door closed. Can't quite work out what happened.

31st March

Went back to 66 Fir Drive today. The lady, Old-Grey-Fur I have named her, was having dinner. She shared her sirloin steak and chips with me. It was wonderful eating REAL food for a change. What a difference from the disgusting tins and packets my humans catch for me. I kept her company for the evening and we both slept for hours on her incredibly soft settee.

I am seriously thinking that I should leave my humans and move in with Old-Grey-Fur.

1st April

(Trickery and Treachery Day - Beware.)

Trousers woke me from a wonderful dream about Snowball, with screams of "Mouse! Mouse!" Running across the carpet was a huge, fierce grey mouse that looked like a cross between a rat and a vacuum cleaner. Being brave and valiant I had to save my humans from this beast. I bounced across the room and, with great precision and dexterity, leapt upon the monster. Clutching the viscous demon between my paws, I held it captive as I rolled over and over. Even when I hit the wall with a mighty thud I held on tight. I looked up, expecting adoration and praise for my heroic act - but everyone was laughing. Only then did I realize it was a plastic clockwork mouse. I had been tricked. What a cheek!

11:00 PM: Caught a mouse in the garden. After snapping off its head I smuggled the pieces into the house. When Trousers and skirt were sound asleep, I left the head and body on their pillows as a nice little surprise.

2nd April

Awoke to the sound of screaming. Spent the day locked in the shed, with no food, liquid refreshments or basic sanitation facilities. Humans are so unfair - they love playing tricks but get all moody if you play a trick on them.

In the shed I had plenty of time to think clever thoughts. Lying under my worry blanket in darkness, it struck me that although cats can see well in the dark, humans go blind when there is no light. Why is this? My theory is that cats' eyes let in dark light as well as light light whereas human's eyes only let in light light.

3rd April

I was allowed back into house but Skirt did not say a word to me all day. Brat on the other hand followed me everywhere, yelling in the most irritating fashion, "Naughty kitty . . . naughty kitty. . . "

Even Brat-2 mocked me by crying, "Whaaaaa, waaaa," every time I passed his pram.

4th April

Skirt spent the whole day 'spring cleaning'. I felt it my duty to help - so I kept well out of her way to let her get on with it. I had breakfast, lunch and dinner with Old-Grey-Fur; she's such a nice human - it's just a pity she smells of fusty old mothballs. Eventually, I couldn't stand the smell any longer and had to go home. Next time I visit, I will freshen up her house by spraying everything.

I must admit that I'm avoiding Snowball in case she asks me again to make friends with Killer. It's not fair, I long to be with her - but I do not long to be mauled to shreds by a manic, malevolent, murdering monster
.

5th April

Today I wrote a profound poem about how unjust the world is:

I love Snowball but hate the world
I fell in love with Snowball,
And all my love did send,
But she won't agree to love only me,
Until I make that absolutely barbarically cruel, detestably evil Killer my friend.

But Killer does not like me,
Oh, it's nothing that he said,
But I can tell by his expression (the bullying, intimidation
and the way he keeps tearing lumps of fur off my back),
He would rather I was dead.

And so I need to choose,
Between love and pain and despair,
And agony and anguish and grief,
And misery and sorrow and torment.
Oh, the world is so unfair.

6th April
(Egg Chasing Sunday.)

This was a fabulous day!!!!!

My humans boiled a batch of eggs and painted them bright colors. Snowball arrived just as they began rolling the eggs in the garden. I jumped on Brat's egg as if it were a mouse. It shattered into a hundred pieces which stuck all over my fur (I must wash later). Brat didn't understand the game and cried. He cried and cried until Skirt boiled and painted another egg.

Trousers threw his egg up high into the air. As it fell Snowball and I charged at it from opposite sides of the garden. We both missed the egg but manage to smash into each other.

Our skulls almost cracked just like the eggs. It was very romantic even though it was incredibly painful. Now I understand what the expression, 'love hurts' means. After that Snowball and I sat under the apple tree and I told her all about my plans to become world famous. She was very impressed and didn't mention Killer even once.

Snowball is fabulous. Love is fabulous. The world is pure brilliant!

7th April

11:44 AM: Feeling happy and full of life I skipped round to see Snowball and asked her to go for a walk in the park. As we walked I felt she was acting strangely. She seemed detached, disinterested and even more aloof than normal.

We stopped at the waste bin and I checked it out for scraps of food. The slugs and snails had got the best bits but I did manage to find some Tandoori Crab and Prawn Curry. Feeling romantic I tried to kiss Snowball but she pushed me away.

"What's up?" I asked.

"Nothing," she replied.

"Nothing?" I quizzed.

"Nothing!" she replied tersely.

And nothing is precisely what she said for the rest of the walk. Girls -they're so complicated.

10:05 PM: I'm feeling miserable and confused.

8th April

Met Lucky today.

"What's nothing?" I asked.

He replied, "Something that has no existence. Something that has no quantitative value. Mathematically, a value that indicates that an object variable is no longer associated with any actual object. Used as an adjective, it refers to something which is insignificant or worthless. In other languages it's, rien, nada, niente and nichts. Or, in other words, naught, nullity, obliteration, oblivion, void, zero, zilch, zip, zippo, zot . . . "

Lucky can be so dumb at times!

Lucky's parrot is unbearable! She claims that Long John Silver was once her human and they sailed to Treasure Island on a ship named Hispaniola. She says that for fun they would attack other ships, steal the valuables and make the ship cats walk the plank. In a voice that is irritating beyond description she kept squawking,

"Aye, aye, me hearties.

We made Adrian walk ze plank.

Shiver me timbers, splish, splash,

Down to Devil's Flea-pit ze dumb cat sank."

I hate that parrot!!

9th April

8:15 AM: Brat has not stopped eating chocolate eggs for days. His chocolaty hand prints now cover every surface. I love chocolate and have licked two doors clean.

9:33 PM: After lunch I rushed to Snowball's house to fix things out. She said that she had nothing to say to me and then spent six hours telling me that I'm inconsiderate and do nothing to please her. She said that I am taking advantage of her good nature by not making friends with Killer. I asked her if she had told Killer to be friends with me and she said I was trying to change the subject. She doesn't want to see me again until I'm Killer's friend. Really! Girls!!

10th April

6:00 AM: I am devastatingly heartbroken. My life is in ruins. There's no point in living any more. But I'm also incredibly hungry. Got Skirt out of bed to serve my breakfast. It was Supreme-of-Synthetic-Wild-Salmon-in-a-Ginger-Soufflé-with-Colouring-Preservatives-Plus-Basil-and-Oregano - surprisingly it almost tasted like real food. I demanded another three portions.

11:59 PM: I was in mourning all day for my lost happiness. Apart from eating and sleeping I did nothing. Due to my insatiable hunger I had eight meals at home and a huge plate of fresh haggis with Old-Grey-Fur. It's odd how sadness makes you hungry - the sadness muscles must be located in the stomach.

11th April

Brat realized that I have become manic depressive and was extra nice to me today. We played chases in the garden all afternoon and, when Brutus barked at me, Brat threw a big branch at him. The silly mutt brought the stick back and Brat threw it at him dozens of times. Unfortunately Brat has a poor aim and didn't hit Brutus once.

Brat-2 is getting bigger by the day and is now eating food that looks exactly the same as mine. I tasted it and it's vile (it's just like tomato and carrot puree - disgusting! - no wonder Brat-2 cries all the time). But I'm so depressed I finished off a bowlful anyway.

12th April
(On this day in 1665 the Great Strike of London began.
Cats in the Mouser's Union refused to kill any rats until
their catnip allowance was increased.)

1:22 PM: Told Lucky all about Snowball insisting I make friends with Killer. He said that someone as clever as me should be able to convince a stupid ruffian like Killer that it would be better if we were friends. It's not often that Lucky says anything sensible but for once he's right.

11:30 PM: My humans have been out all evening. I have been

sitting on my favorite chair having very clever intellectual thoughts. It's good being intelligent; it's such a comfort in times of adversity.
I ran through the 'times-table' I learned as a kitten:

One tail is one.
Two ears are two.
Three mice are tasty.
Four paws are four.
Five dogs are deadly.

I couldn't remember much after that.

13th April

Being an intellectual cat I have written a brilliant speech that will make Killer want to be my friend.

Momentous Speech to Killer
My dear Killer, there is too much pain and suffering in the world. You and I can make it a better place - a paradise for all cats. But we must turn away from hatred and aggression; we must encourage love and friendship amongst catkind. We can do it. We can make a difference and we can start right now by becoming good friends. Let's be friends. What do you say?

Spent the rest of the day practicing my speech - I can now say it without fainting. Will go and see my friend-to-be early tomorrow morning.

14th April

I went to the Lane today but spotted Killer sharpening his claws. I think his father must have been a lion. Will make friends with him some other time.

The Magpie nest in Lucky's garden is growing by the day. I told Lucky that he must be ruthless and destroy it. Summer will be a nightmare if we have to suffer a family of these evil creatures.

15th April

Spent the day in the shed. Think I'm suffering from a syndrome called nerves.

16th April

Plucked up the courage to talk to Killer. Brave, but trembling, I walked down the Lane towards him. I spoke in my most friendly manner, "My dear Killer, there is too much pain and suffering in the world . . . aaarrrghhhhhh . . . oooocccchhhh" Killer dug his claws deep into my face and then slashed my ears until they bled. As I ran back along the Lane he chased after me lashing savagely at my back and tail.

After my attempts at making friends there is even more pain and suffering in the world - mine!!

Trousers added insult to injury, making the pain worse by rubbing my wounds with something called 'antiseptic lotion' - he's so uncaring.

17th April

Snowball had heard about my speech and came round to see my wounds and comfort me. She's such a support when I'm feeling poorly. She must like me ever so much.

In her tender, understanding manner she said, "You must have antagonized Killer - he's a kind, considerate and gentle cat."

"He hates me!" I replied defensively.

"Yes, but in an affectionate way," she insisted.

18th April

(On this day in 1665 the Great Plague of London began. Caused by the rats that overran the city, it killed almost three cats and half the city's humans.)

Brat-2 has a disease called Nappy-Rash. This means that he must cry and get hugs all day.

I can't get a moment's peace to think. With all the stress and complications in my life, this noise is just too much for me to cope with. Must go to my worry blanket.

19th April

10:00 PM: No peace again! Brat-2 is so noisy his tonsils must be breaking the sound barrier.

11:00 PM: To a background of screeching and yelling, I wrote a letter to the Queen:

Dear Queen,

In your Royal Isolation at the Crystal Palace, you are probably unaware of the problems that afflict your subjects. I wish to bring to your attention the fact that there is a terrible outbreak of Nappy-Rash sweeping the country. You may recall that in 1665 the Great Plague wiped out half of London and left the other half guilt ridden for not dying. I feel that if you do not act immediately Nappy-Rash could become the new great plague. It is certainly stopping me from getting any sleep!

Yours Sincerely Adrian Cat.

P.S. While you are fixing the Nappy-Rash problem could you also have Killer hung, drawn and quartered for terrorizing the neighborhood and ruining my love life.

11:50 PM: Placed letter beside the Post Box. It is a very regal red box with the Queen's personal initials carved on the front; **QE 11**. On the back of the box, in yellow paint are the words, 'Big Bob was here.' I expect Big Bob must be one of the Queen's close friends.
She will get my letter soon - it's very exciting.

20th April

*(On this day in 1665 all mousers in London
had their catnip allowance doubled.)*

It's official - I'm suffering from sleep deprivation. Despite all my efforts I got less than the recommended 20 hours daily dose of sleep today. And to make matters worse my humans are all in grumpy moods. I fear that this may be the start of the Nappy-Rash epidemic. It's now too dangerous to remain in the house - tomorrow I leave forever.

21st April

6:22 AM: I packed my bags (or to be more precise I gathered up my most important possessions - a half chewed plastic mouse, a purple feather and two catnip sweeties) and carried them to Old-Grey-Fur's house. After spraying carpets, furniture, teddy bears, electrical appliances, Colt and Winchester gun collection, walls, and Old-Grey-Fur the house smells not so bad. She was delighted to see me and gave me a huge bowl of cream from the fridge. It's so nice to eat good, nutritional food for a change.

7:49 AM: Peace at last

23:45 PM: Not a sound all day (apart from Old-Grey's snoring). Purrfect!!

22nd April

(Day of rest in honor of the Ancient Egyptian Cat Goddess Bast.)

More Peace

23rd April

(Anniversary of the poet Fluffles Shakespeare.)

Still no reply from the Queen. She must be deciding what to do.

It's the anniversary of my favorite poet Fluffles Shakespeare. She was such an original thinker. Each word she wrote was deep and meaningful. Every sentence a poem in itself.

I particularly love this one about a cat in love - I feel as if Fluffles had a window into my heart and captured my emotions:

Half a Sonnet - XI

I wondered lonely as a cat,
In fair Verona, where we lay our scene,
As in the mists of embryonic night,
Thine eyes I love, and they, as pitying me,
O my love is like a red, red rose,
Weary with toil, I haste me to my bed.

24th April

All this peace is giving me the opportunity to think. Intellectuals need to be able to think - that's what makes us intellectuals. I worry a lot about the inequality amongst catkind - it's so unjust that some cats live in the lap of luxury (wearing jeweled collars and eating salmon and cream) - while others roam the streets surviving on scraps from bins. I wish there was something I could do to make life more enjoyable for all cats.

I have come to the conclusion that I am a socialist.

25thApril

I think that Old-Grey-Fur must have feline chromosomes - she sleeps almost as much as I do!

The Magpie nest, in Lucky's garden, has grown so big it could house a family of pigs (if pigs could fly) and must be destroyed. I would climb up and wreck it myself but ever since the Everest Expedition (failed) I have suffered from dendrophobia, the fear of trees. Lucky was nervous at having to destroy the nest himself, but I told him there was no need to worry for I would keep lookout and warn him if the birds returned.

Slowly, and somewhat reluctantly, Lucky climbed the tree and began edging along the narrow branch towards the nest. Diligently, I kept watch. As Lucky reached the nest the branch bent under his weight and he looked very precarious.

"Hurry up slowcoach," I shouted encouragingly.

Lucky climbed into the nest and began the deconstruction work.

Something must have distracted me, for the next thing I knew the Magpies had landed on top of Lucky. They were mighty surprised to find a cat in their nest. The branch was surprised to find a huge nest, a cat and two magpies amongst its leaves and so decided to snap. As Lucky tumbled towards the ground one of the birds did a kamikaze attack into his stomach. It took an hour before Lucky could breath properly again - but at least the mission was accomplished. The nest has been unbuilt.

26th April

Not a sound all day!!

I am going insane!!!

Sometimes the silence is so loud it reverberates around the chambers of my mind making me want to scream just to break the monotony!

I wish Old-Grey-Fur would do something really crazy like smash her teacup against the wall or pull my tail or anything that's not completely boring!

27th April

Moved back in with my humans - they have not yet died from the Nappy-Rash plague. I will put up with their noise, for they need me and a socialist cat should stand by his friends in times of trouble.

My food bowl was piled high with six days worth of food - they hadn't even realize I had left them. My humans always remember to forget me!

28th April

Today I devised a constitution that will enable all cats to live in purr-fect happiness. Now that I have started corresponding with the Queen I'm sure she will make it law.

Cat Constitution.

Freedom of meow.
Freedom to gather at night, for a cats' choir.
Freedom to chase mice.
Freedom from being chased by dogs.
The right to a comfortable home to live in.
The right to have at least one human slave.
The right to six good meals a day.
The right to go in and out of doors whenever we want.
The right to sleep anywhere, anytime.
The right to freely explore every box, drawer, and wardrobe.

29th April

Was shocked to find my letter to the Queen in a puddle beside the Post Box. You would think the Queen would be more respectful than to discard letters in the street. She must realize that I am a socialist and that is why she refuses to reply. Typical of Royalty - they are so Upper-Class!! In future I will deal with her superior, the Prime Minister. He is a Commoner and shares my views.

Brat and I played ball. He threw the ball and I tried to avoid being hit.

30th April

Told Lucky that I am a socialist and explained my Cat Constitution. He was very impressed but said, "Although the Freedom of Meow is sacrosanct in a civilized society it does cause issues due to incompatible values amongst the numerous cat cultures. If there are no restrictions on what cats are allowed to say there is greater opportunity for hatred and intolerance between cats - particularly between different breeds and socio-economic classes. So giving one group liberty means taking it away from weaker groups who are likely to be oppressed."

Really!! Lucky is very clever at thinking stupid things.

Lucky and I are setting out for London tomorrow to get the Prime Minister to make my Cat Constitution law. If I see the Queen I will tell her exactly what I think of her disrespectful behavior.

I am about to become a world famous political activist! That will impress Snowball.

1st May

(Season of Coitus Cravings.)

5:05 AM: Woke up early, with a strange feeling. It's like electricity flowing up through my legs, whizzing around my body, duffing up all my internal organs then shooting out of my whiskers. I can't stop thinking about Snowball and have a great urge to go and see her. In fact, forget breakfast - I'm going right now.

8:40 AM: The streets are full of male cats all acting weird! Some are meowing. Some hissing. Some screeching. But all are walking like zombies, muttering, "girls . . . must find girls." All except Damien, the pretty-boy Ragdoll who wears pink ribbons - he's just looking more bewildered than usual.

Snowball was locked in her house. Her humans insist it's not safe for her to go out for a few days. I tried to smash down the door and nearly cracked my skull.

Jumped in the canal to cool off - but I didn't.

2:00 PM: I eventually found Lucky - wandering the streets aimfully. He said that he wanted to meet a nice girl, get married and settle down - and do so immediately! We went to the park and spotted two girls standing beside the pond.

I told Lucky a great chat-up line, 'How about coming back to my place to see my wallpaper scratchings.' He tried it out on the cute black Bombay cat, (we found out later that she's called Suffragette), but she laughed and said, "Get lost moron or I'll rip your eyes out."

Her friend took a liking for me and began fluttering her eyelashes seductively. She said, "Why don't you come back to my place and try out my purple plastic litter tray." I have never felt so confused, the feelings in my body made me want to kiss this exquisitely ugly feline but my heart wanted me to stay faithful to my much more glamorous true love Snowball.

Eventually my heart won and I came home, leaving Lucky desperately chatting to the girls.

8:00 PM: Have taken six cold baths but still feel very hot and bothered.

11:59 PM: I have not gone to London. I have not become a famous political activist. I am however, very frustrated.

2nd May

Searched all day for Lucky. Couldn't find him anywhere. The streets are still full of zombified cats. I watched twelve of them fighting over a particularly hideous ginger tabby. I would have joined in but they were all much bigger and stronger than me.

The Nappy-Rash plague has stopped - now Brat-2 only cries most of the time.

3rd May

Still can't find Lucky. Tomorrow I will go to London on my own.

4th May

Lucky turned up on my doorstep at 6:06 AM looking absolutely exhausted. He couldn't remember anything about the last two days but he was wearing the silly smile that he keeps for the rare occasions when something good happens to him.

We'll go to London tomorrow - he needs to sleep today. London is 400 miles from Bearsden so it will take several days to get there.

The cold baths have worked at last - my strange feeling has worn off.

5th May

11:24 PM: Great day! I am on my way to being a world famous socialist.

We set out early, and after a long walk through the countryside came to a small town. We found a group of cats standing outside the fishmonger's and I began telling them my plans. Soon dozens of cats had gathered round eager to hear how my Cat Constitution would ensure happiness for all cats. It was so exciting; I felt very important. I just wish Snowball could see me now.

One annoying old, tortoiseshell cat kept demanding that all cats should have the right have at least one toy-mouse to use for mousing practice. Eventually, just to keep her quiet, I told her I would add it to the constitution.

6th May

We walked to the next town and told the cats there about my Cat Constitution. They were all delighted that at last someone is doing something for the downtrodden sleeping class cat, and promised to support us to the death. (I think they meant that metaphorically.)

While I was talking, Susie, a cat we met yesterday, told Lucky that some Fat-Cats are annoyed that we are upsetting the status quo and are coming after us.

We decided it would be best to move on - quickly.

7th May

7:00 AM: Traveled through the night and have reached the next town on our route to London. No sign of the Fat-Cats. We will get some sleep then go to the centre to spread the word.

4:07 PM: We're in hiding! Our lives are in terrible danger!

When we got to the town centre there was already a large group of cats waiting for us. The moment I started talking some trouble makers shouted "trouble maker," and began hissing at me.

Other cats told the trouble makers to be quiet. The trouble makers called them trouble makers too. Soon it became very confusing and every-one was calling everyone else a troublemaker. That's when the fighting broke out - a group of tough Manx cats began clawing and scratching indiscriminately. In the furor, Lucky, Susie and I made a dash for safety. Susie took us to a friend's and we have gone-underground in his shed.

8th May

We are still in the shed hiding from the Fat-Cats and their ruffian henchmen. It has rained non-stop and the roof leaks. I didn't realize that being a political activist would involve so much self-sacrifice, danger, and damp fur.

Susie's friend assures us that we will never be found here.

9th May

6:12 AM: Susie's friend was WRONG.

In the middle of the night the Manx cats broke into the safe shed and took us captive. They dragged us through the darkness, biting and scratching to make us keep walking. We are being kept in a dark, foul smelling cellar until the Fat-Cats arrive. The brutish Manx cats are guarding the door, there is no escape. I think Susie's friend is a traitor! Susie says that the Fat-Cats are likely to hang us by our tails until they stretch to twice their normal length.

10th May

1:05 PM: Eight fierce Fat-Cats arrived and interrogated us - it was awful. They asked hundreds of questions in deep, threatening voices. Nervously, I tried to explain that we didn't mean any harm and all we wanted was for all cats to be happy.

The leader, a three legged Siamese, with a patch over his left eye, said there wasn't enough happiness to go round and that he wasn't going to give up any of his happiness for some dumb little orphan kittens. When I tried to explain that happiness didn't work like that he struck me repeatedly across the face. He wouldn't stop hitting me until I said, "Happiness is the exclusive privilege of the rich," twenty times.

They are now deciding our fate. From the few words I can overhear, I don't think any of my nine lives will be left intact. I will never see Snowball or my humans again.

4:00 PM: A miracle happened! About an hour ago we heard a commotion outside. The Manx guards were agitated and shouted "Keep back or we'll claw your ears off." The noise got louder; we could hear the sound of a large angry mob coming closer and closer. The guards screamed furiously but soon this turned to screeches of fear and pain. Suddenly the cellar door was smashed open and, in the dim light, we saw dozens and dozens of cats piling in through the doorway. A fierce battle ensued in the darkness of the cellar; amidst it all I was grabbed from behind by the Siamese leader. "You will die for your part in this insurgence," he hissed. I was so angry that for a moment I forgot I was a socialist - I lashed out and scratched his good eye. As he reeled back in agony he was clobbered on the head by Susie's friend. Five minutes later, the fighting was over and the Fat-Cats and the guards had fled.

23:35 PM: We spend the evening celebrating. This has been a great victory for all sleeping class cats!

11th May

9:00 AM: Have just discovered that we are in Balloch. We have only traveled twenty miles - and in the wrong direction. London is now 420 miles away. I have decided to go home. Being a political revolutionary is too difficult for someone with poor navigational skills.

9:10 PM: Back home. I am finished with politics forever. I will find a less radical way to become famous.

11:46 PM: My humans have been playing a card game called 'snap' all evening. They spend endless hours doing this - they have no ambition. They really are a big disappointment to me.

12th May

Walked with Trousers to his office. He obviously enjoyed the company, for as soon as we got there he picked me up and carried me all the way home.

Brutus is as grumpy as ever! I lay by the garden fence and taunted him with jeers of, "snot face, snot face." It was fun to watch him straining at his leash in an effort to get at me. He's such a stupid brute! On the evolutionary scale, dogs are just ahead of crustaceans.

13th May

Spent today with Lucky. He is madly in love with Suffragette. But when he goes to see her she tells him to 'get lost' and punches him - I don't think this is a good sign. Lucky is hopeless with girls - he really needs my help - big time.

Have not seen Snowball for so long I think my heart is fading away from lack of love.

14th May

Played a great game with Skirt in the garden. She planted bulbs and I dug them up again. I could have played for hours if she hadn't locked me in the house.

15th May

Snowball turned up unexpectedly and invited me for a walk along the canal. We walked and talked and kissed for ages - it was brilliant. She had heard about my London adventure and is very proud of me. She says she will be even more proud when I am rich and powerful. She insists that having an influential ally like Killer would help me become famous and that then I will be able to give her all the things she wants. I reminded her that Killer didn't want to be my friend but she just smiled and said that she would fix that.

I didn't realize vegetarians could be so single-mindedly ambitious.

16th May

(St. Whiskas Day - Patron Saint of Overindulgence.)

When I awoke this morning the living room was full of brightly colored parcels. I was very excited. I love opening parcels. I love ripping paper too. But the moment I started, Skirt came rushing in yelling "bad boy." I think "bad boy" translates into Cat-Language as "go for it" so it was confusing that she was telling me to tear open the parcels and at the same time hitting me with a towel. Humans never know what they want!

Brat came to help me open the presents - Skirt didn't hit him with the towel. It took ages to unwrap everything but I am please to report that I got; a big blue ball, a toy car, a red plastic gun, a cuddly purple teddy bear, a tin of sticky tacky bouncy rubbery stuff, two jumpers, a pair of shoes and four big boxes with unidentifiable things in them. I have no use for the jumpers and shoes, so Brat can have these.

I scooped out the contents of the biggest box and spent an hour exploring the inside. Boxes are fascinating - they seem to posses mysterious qualities - I think one day it will be discovered that they contain secret portals into cat utopia.

Trillions of Brat's friends came to the house and we had a brilliant party. The best part was bursting the balloons. I was best at it. The final balloon-bursting score was Me 8 - Brat's Friends 1. The girl with the yellow dress got so excited when I burst her balloon that she cried until *she* nearly burst. Skirt served up big dishes of ice-cream and jelly but forgot to give me one. I ate as much as I could steal from the plates and am now so full I need to sleep. It has been a fun day!

Brat had a fun day too - he was sick all over his bedroom carpet.

17th May

Had a serious accident today!! I sat on one of Brat-2's nappies only to discover that it was dirty.

I have washed 42 times but still smell of poo.

18th May

I asked Snowball how Lucky could impress Suffragette and win her affection - being a girl she knows these things. She said that the way to a girl's heart is through her cravings for material possessions. She said that all girls love getting presents.

19th May

Visited Old-Grey-Fur as I haven't seen her for days. Went at lunch time. She was so pleased to see me she gave me half of her lunch - I got the biggest half.

20th May

Lucky and I played tease with Brutus. We sat at the fence and called him dog-breath, dog-ugly, dog-ears, dog-face, dog-tired and all sorts of dog-horrible names. Brutus has no sense of humor; he got furious and ran about yelping, pulling at his leash in an effort to reach us. We laughed so much I coughed up a fur-ball. Our fun was brought to an abrupt end when his leash broke and he leapt over the fence. Fortunately we managed to scramble onto the shed roof or we would have been ripped to shreds. We were stuck there for hours, with Brutus snarling up at us like a blood-thirsty werewolf, before we were finally rescued. It's awful not being safe in your own garden.

21st May

My humans took me to a cat beautician today. She brushed and trimmed my fur, gave me a shampoo with lots of bubbles, then clipped and smoothed my claws. It was quite good fun but I'm not going to tell Snowball or Lucky about it.

22nd May

Snowball wanted to do something romantic so I took her to my very favorite place - the Council Dump. I love watching the huge machines pushing the heaps of rubbish and adore the wonderful aroma that fills your every breath. Snowball was so overawed that she didn't say much - in fact she got so emotional she could hardly breathe and we had to come away. But later she said something rather odd - she said, "Training you is going to be a bigger challenge than I imagined." I wonder what she meant!

23rd May

Lucky and I made a present for Suffragette. We attached dandelion flowers and a piece of shiny silver paper to an old collar I had found at the Dump. It looks really good - Lucky will give it to her later and win her heart. Lucky is lucky having a good friend like me to help him.

24th May

Hurried round to Lucky's to find out how he got on yesterday. He had a black eye, a cut ear, and a badly bruised ego. He said that Suffragette is a feminist but I'm not sure what that means.

25th May
(Anniversary of the invention of fresh tinned salmon.)

11:49 PM: Overslept today - have just woken. Will get a bite to eat then take a nap.

26th May

My duty as Protector of Territory is extremely onerous. Today I had to chase away eight birds, six bees, three butterflies and a ladybird without the slightest help from my humans.

Snowball took me to her favorite place; a quiet spot in the park that is overgrown with tulips. We lay together surrounded by flowers and kissed. I prefer the fragrance of the Dump to the smell of tulips but Snowball seemed happy. She said that when I'm famous she's going to marry me and have my kittens. Funny - I don't remember asking her to marry me!

27th May

1:00 PM: My humans have gone out leaving me to look after the house.
4:20 PM: I am bursting for a pee but my litter tray has been missing since Skirt's latest cleaning frenzy.

5:05 PM: Searched the house to find a place to pee that won't leave too much of a mess. The video-thing seemed a good choice.

11:00 PM: Trousers is in a dreadful mood because the video-thing won't work. I don't know why he's angry at me when really it's all Skirt's fault.

28th May

9:20 PM: Thought I'd sleep on Brat's bed for a change. Climbed up and discovered there were lots of bed mice running about under the blankets. Dived on one but missed. Dived again and missed. Dived again and again and again and again but couldn't catch any of them. Brat was no help - he was too busy laughing. I can't understand why bed mice are impossible to catch. The strangest thing of all was that whenever I crawled under the duvet, the mice vanished! Eventually I was so exhausted and embarrassed I went to the kitchen to sleep.

29th May

7:00 AM: Trousers and Skirt are in a bad mood just because during the night I demanded to be let out four times and let in seven times. (I often change my mind about these things at the very last moment.)

8:00 PM: Have been thinking about why humans get so upset about doors; to them 'out' and 'in' are opposites. But we cats often want to be out and in at same time. For cats 'out' and 'in' are exactly the same – just separated by a door.

11:20 PM: Tried to demonstrate my theory on doors by going in and out repeatedly but my humans are too dumb to understand.

30th May

Had great fun chasing a mouse all along the alley. Eventually it escaped, absentmindedly leaving its tail in my mouth. I thought the tail would make a nice present for Old-Grey-Fur as she has been so kind to me. I placed it on a chair and sat back to watch her surprise and joy. Would you believe it! She tried to darn some socks with it! She's a funny old thing!

31st May

(Cats' Eyes invented on this day in 1936 - no cats were injured, experimented upon, or mildly tortured in the development of these devices.)

Snowball and I talked about our future together. Well, to be more precise, she talked all day about her future but I think she mentioned me once or twice.

After she kissed me goodnight, I watched her squeeze through the rose bushes and stomp over our neighbor's lettuces. She's perfect in every way; beautiful, charming, caring, loving, kind, tolerant and unselfish. I am the happiest cat in the universe

Perhaps we will get married one day.

1st June

11:23 PM: The house is in complete darkness. Everyone is asleep. There is a noise coming from the attic; a strange spooky sort of noise like tiny little banshees dragging tiny little chains across tiny little grave-stones. Not the sort of noise I like to hear when my humans are all asleep. Strange noises in the dark don't worry me but I'm going to climb into bed beside Trousers and Skirt and try not to think about it.

2nd June

Wonderful sunny day. Lay in the garden enjoying the heat. Brat was running around chaotically kicking a ball. I would have joined in but knew if I made even the slightest movement the sun would stop shining.

3rd June

11:30 AM: Lucky is feeling dejected. He loves Suffragette uncon-ditionally. She hates him unconditionally. Love may be blind but unrequit-ed love beats up your heart with its white walking cane. Once more Lucky needs my guidance. I explained that humor is a great way to win a girl's adoration and told him a brilliant joke to use:

"What do you get if you cross a flea, a chicken and a kangaroo?
An omelet that can jump over houses."

Lucky laughed until he was sick. Making Suffragette laugh is a sure way to win her affection.

2:20 PM: Lucky told Suffragette my joke. She didn't even smile. He's absolutely useless at telling jokes.

It's a shame that Lucky's love life is so disastrous while mine is so perfectly wonderful.

4th June
(St Puskin's Day - Patron Saint of Sleep.)

Killer turned up in my garden! He said he wants to be my friend!!!

5th June

Snowball and I went to the beach - it was absolutely crowded. We tried to walk along the water's edge but kept getting splashed. Humans obviously find paddling very tiring for the beach was covered in people lying half comatose on their backs. Eventually we found a reasonably quiet spot in the long grass between discarded polystyrene burger containers. Out of respect for Snowball's religion of vegetarianism, I overcame my desire to eat the mouth-watering scraps of burger. We chatted for what seemed like a wistful eternity. When I told her about Killer she smiled and said she knew everything would work out. I was so happy I wanted to say, 'I love you,' but every time I tried I got fur-balls in my throat.

6th June

4:00 PM: I'm rather concerned about Brat-2; he still gets pushed everywhere in his buggy. By this time a cat kitten would be climbing trees and catching mice. Human kittens are such slow developers.

I tried to write a love poem but my brain was obviously not working properly - the only lines I could think of were quite useless:

She Loves You
She loves you, yeah, yeah, yeah
She loves you, yeah, yeah, yeah

And with a love like that
You know you should be glad.

11:40 PM: Heard the spooky noise again - I wonder if the house was built on a graveyard.

7th June

11:00 AM: Skirt has been calling me for the last ten minutes. She seems to think I'll come running at her every whim just like a dog. I have a huge amount to write into my diary so she'll just have to wait until I'm ready . . . oohh she's shouting, 'din dins' must go . . .

8th June

While Lucky and I were lazing under the rose bushes, Killer crept up. He said that we are to meet him by the pond in the park tomorrow morning. I'm glad we are friends but I do wish he wouldn't come into my garden - it makes me feel insecure.

9th June

We all met at the pond and had a great day. Killer could not have been friendlier. He was all smiles and jokes and didn't maul me even once. However, he's obviously not very intelligent for every other word he says is "meoomea" or "mieowooo". I think he would get on well with Trousers.

10th June

5:00 PM: Brat and I played in the garden all day. First we played catch-worm. I ate five, he only ate three. Next we played in our paddling pool; he kept jumping in creating huge splashes and I ran like crazy to avoid being soaked. Then he carried me to the top of our slide to let me slide down it. It's not as easy as it looks; I rolled down head over paws and ended up in the pool. We stopped playing then.

6:00 PM: Brat has gone all red! Skirt has covered all the red patches with white stuff to take away the pain. She hasn't put any on me even though it was me who fell off the slide into the pool!

11th June

I visited Snowball today, determined to tell her how much I love her. But before I could say a word she told me that I'm getting fat and need to diet and take more exercise.

I'm not really fat for my size but I'd do anything for Snowball. I will delay telling her I love her until I am completely unfat.

12th June

(On this day in 1858 the can opener was invented. One that can be operated by cats has so far defeated human intelligence!)

Too warm to do anything today. I lay under the rosebushes and created a list of my top thousand sleeping places. Here are a few:

On Skirt's expensive satin ball gown.
On Trousers' prize winning flowers.
In the heat of any sunbeam.

Under hedges with the slugs, worms and cockroaches.
In the middle of a pile of newly washed towels.
Anywhere Trousers wants to sit.

13th June

Heard the spooky noise again. My hair stood on end. It's a well documented fact that if a cat's hair stands on end there's a ghost present!

Too afraid to be in by myself - spent the afternoon with Old-Grey-Fur.

14th June

11:20 AM: Snowball has given me a diet and exercise plan. Each day I must:

Walk 2 kilometers.
Jump on and off a chair 20 times.
Eat only two meals.

She must really, really like me a lot to go to all the trouble of creating this nutritionally balanced plan.

7:50 PM: I asked Lucky if he believes in ghosts. He replied, "Belief is merely the affirmation of, or a conviction regarding, the truth of a proposition, especially when one is not in possession of evidence adequate to justify a claim that the proposition is known with certainty. What you really wish to know is the probability of ghosts existing. Using Bayesian Paradigm for statistical inference it is possible to create a probability distribution based on data from tests and observations which allows the inference about the value of the true unknown. In the case of ghosts the probability distribution indicates that the likelihood of there being ghosts is somewhere between, 'Don't be stupid!' and 'Aaaaaarrgghhh! Help! My body has been possessed by an evil demon!'" What nonsense, sometimes Lucky says what he doesn't mean.

15th June

Killer, Snowball and I found an old door floating on the canal and used it as a raft. I was given the important task of paddling while Killer and Snowball navigated.

Snowball kept shouting, "Faster slave, faster" even though I was paddling as fast as my paws could go. After a while Killer offered to help but he's so clumsy that, while paddling, he accidentally kicked me. With a huge splash, I found myself in the middle of the canal. By the time I'd struggled to the bank, the raft was out of sight. I came home to get dried out and didn't see Snowball or Killer for the rest of the day.

Ate eight big meals and a spider today.

16th June

2:00 PM: Met Snowball in the park. She said they had a great time yesterday and it was a pity that I had decided not to stay. She asked about my diet. I told her it was going as well as could be expected.

11:20 PM: The noise is back again. My humans heard it too, so it really is a ghost and not just my imagination.

17th June

10:00 AM: A van with the words, 'Rat Busters' written across it, has arrived at my house.

11:20 AM: Two men have been in the attic for ages looking for the ghosts.

11:48 PM: The ghosts have gone!!! (Though, of course, I don't really believe in ghosts.)

11:55 PM: I stuck to my diet plan today. I am almost a skeleton.

18th June

I lay under the sycamore and thought about the division of tasks in my household.

Skirt washes, irons, worries, scrubs, cooks, and vacuums.

Trousers fixes the car, paints doors and arranges stamps in a big album.

Brat builds things with blocks and knocks them down again.

Brat-2 makes smells and noises.

And I need to do the dangerous task of protecting the property from rats, wasps, mice, squirrels, birds, serial killers, bees, flies and a mass of other intruders.

It's so unfair that the largest burden falls on me.

19th June

Trousers was reading a letter marked 'Rat Busters - Bill' and using those strange words again. He said angrily, "What's the point of having a cat if he can't even catch a few dumb mice - it's time to get rid of him."

What a cheek! I'm the best mouser in the world - no mouse is safe within a mile of me without a life insurance policy!!

20th June

Killer insisted that we explore the railway today. I've never been there before, for it's such a dangerous place. But Killer says that it's perfectly safe if you know what you're doing. We climbed across lots of track and went into old engines and carriages. It was great fun. Then Killer showed me how to climb onto the arches above the carriage wheels. Unfortunately he chose a train that was about to move. I had to cling on with all my might as the train sped along at top speed with the track whizzing by inches below me. I have never been so scared. The train didn't stop for miles and it took me hours to find my way home. At least I got plenty of exercise today. Poor Killer will be so embarrassed at his mistake.

21st June
(Longest Day - perfect for taking extra long naps.)

Rained all day, with lots of thunder and lightening.
I stayed indoors - under the bed.

22nd June

Snowball came round to check how my diet is going. I'm wasting away to nothing but she says I've put on more weight - she has increased my exercises and reduced the size of my meal portions. I said that I would starve to death but she said I can drink as much water as I want.

23rd June

7:30 AM: Overheard Trouser saying, "That good-for-nothing cat is costing us a fortune - he's got to go." Not sure who they were talking about but it made me think that I'd better prove what a great mouser I am.

10:10 AM: Caught a young mouse in the alley. Her name is Squeeeek and she seems quite bright. I explained that she had two choices:

a) Being hung, drawn, quartered, and then eaten.

b) Helping me trick my humans.

Fortunately for her she chose the latter option.

4:00 PM: After lots of rehearsing we were ready. Squeeeek ran across the carpet. Skirt screamed and jumped onto a chair. Squeeeek danced in front of the chair (though I thought her dying swan ballet routine was a bit overacted) I rushed in to save Skirt, grabbed Squeeeek by the tail and carried her out of the house. I have promised Squeeeek a regular supply of cheese to repeat the performance once a month.

11:00 PM: I got extra, extra, extra servings of food today. Oooops! I forgot my diet!

24th June

I ate so much yesterday I had to sleep all day to recover.

25th June

8:30 AM: Pulled petals off roses, saying the rhyme 'She-Loves-Me, She-Loves-Me-Not' to find out if Snowball really does love me. I had to use forty-two roses before it turned out She-Loves-Me but at least I now have scientific proof that she does.

9:00 AM: Skirt came in from the garden looking puzzled. She said to Trousers, "There must have been a hurricane this morning." Strange - there was no wind when I was out.

4:00 PM: Went to see Snowball; her humans are so cute - they kept trying to feed me. Snowball had to remind me several times about my diet. Her humans said to each other, "Wouldn't it be nice if this lovely pair had kittens." Now that I know Snowball loves me, I tend to agree.

26th June

If I'm to be a father I need to get into shape. Did two lots of exercise and ate two lots of food.

Brat thought it was funny seeing me jump up and down on the chair and joined in. He wasn't as good as me and Skirt put a plaster on his head.

27th June

Really hot today. Snowball, Lucky, Killer and I lazed on top of the bins in the alley for ages until Killer suggested playing Truth-or-Dare. When Snowball chose Truth, I asked her who she loves. She thought for a while then replied, "I could only ever love a wise, powerful, ruthless, ambitious, famous cat." As this describes me precisely I was ecstatic.

Killer dared me to run to the Sewage Works and back in less than five minutes. This was a dumb dare for it took me over an hour running my fastest. When I got back Snowball and Killer were gone.

Lucky says that Killer is evil and I should stop being friends with him. He's wrong - I'm beginning to like Killer.

28th June

11:45 AM: Lucky was very pleased with himself this morning - he had visited Suffragette and she hadn't told him to get lost or hit him. My advice on love is obviously working!

5:10 PM: Brat-2 is playing the bubble game. He likes to lie in his cot blowing milky bubbles until lots of yellow liquid comes spewing out of his mouth.

29th June

11:55 PM: Something has been troubling me. I have agreed to eat only two meals a day but what if I catch twenty mice - is that one meal or twenty. And what if I steal three fish from the fishmonger?

11:58 PM: I have solved the problem - I have given up my diet.

30th June

8:00 PM: Lazed in the garden all day with Snowball. I wanted to be completely truthful about my diet so I didn't mention that I've given up. It was too hot to do anything except sleep, kiss and check each other for fleas.

1st July

11:00 AM: Trousers grabbed me by surprise while I was eating, squashed me into a basket, and took me to the vet. (I have never understood why vets have such a disliking for cats - when all other humans find us adorable!) Before I could scratch the sadistic brute, he plunged a huge needle-of-death into my neck. I am dying. I'll never forgive Trousers for this!

11:59 PM: I am not dead yet.

2nd July

Brat-2 is getting bigger and stronger by the day. Now he can hit me with a rusk from 3 meters.

Killer told me that I am to become one of his best friends and insisted that I join his gang. He has quickly taken a liking for me and obviously respects and trusts me. Pity this has happened just as I'm about to die.

11:59 PM: I am still not dead.

3rd July

Told Snowball about joining Killer's gang. She was delighted. To celebrate we went to the Sewage Works and watched the rats swimming in the sludge.

Trousers and I had a misunderstanding with the newspaper. He thought he was reading it and I knew we were playing a paper tearing game.

11:59 PM: Death is a slow process.

4th July

Lucky arrived at the door in an uncharacteristic state of overexcitement. "Come see, quick, come see," he gasped.

We ran all the way to Suffragette's house. What a surprise; she has six kittens. Even more of a surprise is that the kittens look like a mixture of Lucky and Suffragette. Suffragette introduced me to each one; Hucky, Rucky, Mucky, Ducky, Zucky and the smallest Yucky. Their eyes are not open yet but what a noise they make.

Suffragette and Lucky were so happy they accidentally kissed each other.

When I told Snowball about the kittens she said, "Having two kittens is almost acceptable but having six is so proletarian."

5th July

Killer introduced me to the members of his gang, Satan, Scarface, Snapbone and Rosepetal. They all seem very nice. I asked Snapbone how he got such an odd name. "Don't know," he replied pensively, "sometimes they go crunch rather than snap!"

Killer said that his gang is called Cosa Nostra and while the gang's together I am to call him Capo.

In a few days time we are all meeting up for an initiation ceremony. I'm looking forward to that.

I was right about Killer; he's kind at heart - he just hides it with his harsh outward aggression.

6th July

Being part of Killer's gang makes me feel important. When cats rule the world, and I am extremely powerful, my laws will be:

Emperor Adrian's Laws

Humans will continue to be our slaves.

Vets will be banned.

Bowls will always be full and litter trays empty.

Dogs will be small and fun to chase.

Mice will come in a variety of flavors.

Tins will not have lids.

There will be 42 hours in each day to allow more time for sleeping.

7thJuly

(Anniversary of Isaac-Flufkins Newton discovering gravity.)

Read about Newton; One day he was sitting under an apple tree when a rather fat cat fell from a branch and landed beside him. Newton observed that the cat landed on all four paws. After conducting many experiments that involved throwing different breeds of cats off a number of tall structures, Newton concluded that cats always land on all four paws. He called this invention gravity. I think I will invent something brilliant!!

Polly has taken to landing on Lucky's back and squawking, "I claim this ship as me own me hearties - we set sail for France at sundown."
Lucky finds this infuriating as a) he is not a ship, b) if he was a ship he would not be Polly's ship c) if he was Polly's ship he would not wish to sail to France.

For Lucky's sake, I need to sort out that annoying parrot!!

8th July

Went to see Suffragette and Lucky. The kittens are gorgeous!
Ducky is almost all black with one small spot of white on her head. She looks most like her mum.

Yucky is black with a few spots of white on his body and tail.

Zucky has black and white stripes and looks like a zebra.

Hucky, Rucky, and Mucky have equal amounts of black and white exactly like Lucky.

They suckle constantly and Lucky runs about crazy catching mice to feed Suffragette - this is particularly stupid as her humans arrive every ten minutes with another bowl of food.

9th July

Met the Cosa Nostra gang for the initiation ceremony. Killer, sorry Capo, said it involved walking over the Erskine Bridge. This sounded fun. What I didn't realize until we got to the bridge is that I was to walk across the girders of the bridge - the bridge is a mile long and the girders just 10 cm wide!

As I shivered and quaked my way across, with the deadly River Clyde fifty meters below, I couldn't stop thinking, "if Newton is right, when I fall and hit the water I'll die paws first."

I didn't fall off the bridge, so I'm now a member of the gang. I feel very privileged, important and still alive.

10th July

Snowball says I look more sophisticated now that I'm part of Killer's gang. We kissed so much that I almost coughed up the mouse I'd eaten earlier.

11th July

Today's the day I teach Lucky and Polly some important lessons. I'll show Polly that he can't mess with cats - especially with an influential member of the Cosa Nostra. At the same time I'll show Lucky how to deal with pesky pirate parrots.

As Lucky watched eagerly from the doorway, I crept stealthily across the room. Polly saw nothing as I made my way silently past her perch, jumped onto a chair and climbed to the top of the bookcase. Polly sat on her perch below me, oblivious to the fact that she was about to be pulverized.

I prepared myself mentally for the attack, crouched down, and leapt with all my might. But just as I was about to land on top of her, she decided to fly round the room. Frantically I tried to grab her but landed on the perch instead. I balanced precariously on the narrow bar, wondering what had gone wrong with my plan. It was at this precise moment in time that Lucky's humans elected to enter the room. They stared at me as if I was some sort of mass murderer. To make matters worse, Polly landed beside me, pecked me gently on the mouth, and squealed, "Polly has a boyfriend. Adrian loves Polly." How embarrassing,

My humans have been extra, extra, extra nice to me. Perhaps they sense my new status as an important gang member.

12th July

5:00 PM: The kittens have all opened their eyes. They're so cute. Yucky is my favorite - he's the smallest yet he keeps dive-bombing the others. It's fun to watch them pile on top of each other like spaghetti with vicious teeth and claws.

8:00 PM: My humans are putting all their possessions into large cases! Already they have packed most of their clothes and loads of toys and they're still scurrying about taking things out of cupboards and drawers. I'm going to check whether they've put the kitchen sink in yet.

11:00 PM: Trousers fed me sweeties while I relaxed on Skirt's lap. Something strange is going on - I hope they are not in some sort of trouble.

13th July

(On this day in 1785 the claw sharpening device, wallpaper, was invented.)

Our gang met at Sycamore Drive. Capo said we were going to break into number thirty-three and steal their valuables. While Killer, Satan, Scarface, and Snapbone kept lookout, Rosepetal and I sneaked in through an open window and ransacked the place. I got a brilliant plastic duck and a superb woolly-blue-thingy-with-a-small-tinkly-bell. Rosepetal stole some gold colored sparkly things from a box marked 'Antique Jewelry' - this stuff may be of interest to humans but it's of no value to cats. Rosepetal is a useless thief! Our haul was given to Capo who looks after all the gang's swag.

Burglary was very exciting but I do feel very guilty about stealing such precious things.

I wonder if you can still be an Intellectual if you are a Burglar.

14th July

11:45 AM: Snowball was to meet me to see the kittens but she didn't turn up.

7:00 PM: Went to see Snowball this afternoon. It's a bizarre coincidence; she has a plastic duck and a woolly-blue-thingy-with-a-small-tinkly-bell just like the ones I stole last night.

When I asked why she hadn't come with me to see the kittens, she said that they bring tears to her eyes. I thought this was so sentimental of her - until she added, "I seem to have an allergy to the disgusting little beasts."

15th July

6:00 PM: My humans are *still* packing cases!! I climbed into one and fell asleep amidst a pile of underwear. Some idiot closed the case and I was stuck there for hours. Fortunately underwear is very absorbent and soaked up all my pee - so I was quite comfortable.

8:00 PM: My humans are still being affectionate - every time I move they try to feed me, stroke me or both - it's becoming rather irritating.

11:40 PM: Snowball and I sat on the bins and watched the moonrise. I hadn't realized you can see the Gasworks from the alley - with the moonlight glistening off the rusting pipes it looks terrific. Being in love opens your eyes to the beauty around you. I wish this evening could have lasted forever. My life is perfect.

16th July

10:00 AM: No! No! No! This can't be happening! Someone must have grassed on me! I've been thrown into prison! It's called Cattery-Prison and it's a grim, dark place; from my tiny cell I can see row upon row of cells, each one filled with an evil, hardened criminal. This is a nightmare. I'd cry but I'm afraid the other inmates will hear and think that I'm weak.

4:25 PM: During exercise break I was allowed out of my cell and was able to walk around the securely fenced exercise area. There were a number of other inmates there too. I was rather nervous that one might attack me but everyone was very civilized. I expect criminals have a code of honor. I met a pretty, grey Tonkinese called Duno Wong. She doesn't look like a criminal but she admitted that a few days before being detained she had climbed onto the kitchen table and eaten a huge cream cake. Her humans must have shopped her - how terribly uncaring.

We spoke in hushed voices so as not to attract the attention of the guard.

"What are you in for?" she whispered.

"Stealing a woolly-blue-thingy-with-a-small-tinkly-bell." I replied.

"Why did you steal that?" she asked, in an almost mocking voice.

"Everything has its purpose," I replied coolly, not wanting to reveal that I am part of an organized criminal gang.

She told me that no one has had a trial or knows for how long they are to be imprisoned.

11:55 PM: I can't sleep. I'm too scared. There could be a murderer in the next cell for all I know! I wish I could climb into my warm, cozy bed and cuddle up against my humans. Life is so unjust!

17th July

9:00 AM: Was woken out of a beautiful dream in which Snowball and I were married and living with the Queen. As we lay on her Queen sized bed she fed us caviar and kept apologizing for dropping my letter in the puddle.

The guards are going from cell to cell giving everyone their rations. For a prison the food isn't bad.

5:40 PM: I met Morgan during exercise. He's a rather scruffy looking cat of mixed breeding who comes from the rough side of town. This is his third stint inside - he's a hardened criminal. Clearly the penal system is not working. This time he's in for pooing in his human's bed moments before she climbed in.

Morgan told me that organized crime is going on right under the guards' noses. Apparently there's trafficking in catnip, chocolate mice and all sorts of things. He says that for a collar you can get three dead sparrows. If only

I had known I was to be imprisoned, I could have brought things to trade - but I have nothing so I won't get any luxuries while I'm here.

5:58 PM: Just before our cells were locked Morgan gave me some catnip - how kind of him.

18th July

Morgan introduced me to Macavity. He's a long-timer. He's been in for four weeks. He instantly recognized me as an intellectual and invited me to join his escape committee. I did. Six of us spent our exercise time discussing ways to break out. It was agreed that digging would be too difficult and anyway Allwhite voted against it as it would make her fur dirty. Cutting through the cell bars is impossible, they are far too strong - several inmates have broken claws on them already. While we were talking, a cat called Houdini approached us. He had heard a rumor that we were planning to breakout. He claimed that no lock could hold him and promised that, if we let him join us, he would get us all out. After a long discussion it was agreed that there were already too many in the escape committee. We meet again tomorrow.

19th July

10:00 AM: Had a chat with the prisoner in the cell to my left. She's in for scratching wallpaper. She's completely distraught. At home she only ever eats table-scraps and now she's being forced to eat Faux-Venison-with-Caviar-Substitute-in-a-Roast-Nutmeg-Sauce - a severe punishment indeed.

I expect that Snowball is pining for me. I hope she's not too miserable but in a way I hope she is.

5:00 PM: Macavity has devised a brilliant plan which is sure to work. He has paid two cats to start a fight when the guard enters the room.

During the distraction we'll make a run for the open door and be free before the guard realizes what's happened.

It's great to know that in just a day or two I will be free again! I am missing Snowball more than a tree misses its leaves in autumn.

20th July

9:30 AM: A new cat has just been brought in, crying dreadfully and protesting her innocence. As the guards locked her in her cell she kept shouting that she hadn't done anything wrong. A likely story.

10:44 AM: She's still crying.

1:30 PM: I spoke to the new inmate. Her name is Princess - she's a beautiful ginger Abyssinian. She acts and talks rather snootily but otherwise seems nice. To cheer her up I told her about Suffragette, Lucky and all the kittens. At last I got her to stop crying and even managed to make her smile. She told me that she enters cat competitions all over the country and has won lots and lots of prizes. She's terrified that while she's in here her fur will not be groomed properly and she'll never be able to enter another show.

4:45 PM: Macavity is making the final arrangements for the escape. We go tomorrow.

21st July

9:00 AM: I'm feeling very nervous. If we get caught we could be put into solitary - or worse!

4:50 PM: I am not free - there was a serious hitch.

Everything seemed to be going to plan; the two cats fought and the guard went to stop them, leaving the door open. We all ran through, thinking freedom would soon be ours. What we didn't realize is that beyond the door there's a long corridor and then another door. As we all rushed through the first door a guard came in through the second. Macavity jumped at him, scratched his arm, and scrambled through the door before it was slammed shut. But the rest of us were trapped. Minutes later we were all bundled back into our cells. I await my punishment.

22nd July

10:00 AM: So far I have not been punished. The guards in here are experts in mental cruelty. No doubt, when I'm least expecting it, they'll slam me into solitary and leave me on my own for days, without food, water or any form of intellectual stimulation. I can't bear the tension of not knowing what's going to happen.

10:50 AM: Macavity has been caught! He's back in his cell!

1:40 PM: Macavity explained that he couldn't remember his way home. He walked non stop all day and night. In the morning, exhausted and hungry, he sneaked into a house to steal food. But the silly thing had walked round in a circle and broken into the guard house next to Cattery-Prison.

2:12 PM: Houdini and four other cats mysteriously disappeared this afternoon!!!

23rd July

3:00 PM: We were all feeling rather subdued today after the failed breakout. Still no sign of Houdini and his friends. A lady came into the prison and spend hours grooming Princess. She was so happy she couldn't stop purring.

I wish I could be happy. I wish I could be with Snowball. I wish I could see the kittens. I wish I could be back with my friends Lucky and

Killer. I wish I could scratch Trousers for allowing me to be put in this awful place!

11:59 PM: A few hours ago, the guards put Macavity into a basket and took him away - he has not returned. I think he's been given the death-penalty.

24th July

(70 years since scientist Professor Whizkats invented faux cat food. Sadly Whizkats died of food poisoning a few days later.)

10:05 PM: What a day! My emotions have been put through the washing machine, dish washer and tumble drier!

In the morning I was grabbed from my cell and put into a basket. I was sure I was going to be given the death-penalty. As I was carried through the prison my heart fluttered uncontrollably. Two thoughts dominated my mind; in a civilized society, was the barbaric death-penalty acceptable - even for a heinous crime like stealing a woolly-blue-thingy-with-a-small-tinkly-bell then trying to escape from prison? and was I too late to call my lawyer?

But when the basket was opened I was in my humans' car - not in the death-penalty room. They were all excited to see me. I was so ecstatic I peed all over Skirt - but she just laughed.

Soon we were home again. Brat was so happy to have me back he gave me lots of presents - the best one is a pink-mouse-on-a-string. For the rest of the day Trousers and Skirt took all the things out of the cases again while Brat and I played chases with my new pink mouse.

It's so good to be free again.

25th July

Rushed round to see Snowball.

"I'm back, I'm back," I cried, all out of breath, "have you missed me terribly?"

"Have you been somewhere?" she asked rather insensitively. "I hadn't noticed."

I told her about being locked in prison for stealing the woolly-blue-thingy-with-a-small-tinkly-bell.

She said, "You have such a lot to learn - Killer would never get caught."

After that we walked along the canal and I told her all about prison. She wanted to know every detail - especially about Princess.

"I think I could be a top model and win lots of prizes at shows," she said modestly.

I agreed, but I must admit I was rather disappointed that she hadn't missed me even a little. I guess she must have been very busy and that's why.

26th July

7:30 PM Lucky is spending most of his time helping with the kittens. They are a bit of a handful so today I helped out. Cats have an inborn desire for adventure - the kittens are constantly trying to escape from the garden. They'll squeeze through even the smallest of gaps. It took all three of us to stop them running away. They also fight relentlessly. Ducky is the champion - she has a punch just like her mother. At one point she hit me in the eye - but I think it was an accident.

11:00 PM: Made a stupid mistake. Heard a rat like noise coming from the rose bushes. I took to the ground and slowly edged towards it, getting as close as possible without being seen. I lay in silence and waited. Its dark shape gradually came within pouncing distance.

I jumped. I grabbed. I cried, "Aaaaaaaaghhhhhhh!!!"

It was a hedgehog - a particularly prickly one.

"Sorry," he said apologetically, as I tried to extract his needle-like spines from my paws and stomach, "but you really should be more careful."

11:58 PM: I'm still aching from the hedgehog attack. But even worse than that - I've got fleas from somewhere.

27th July

7:00 AM: Woke up early, feeling sickeningly itchy all over. Couldn't get back to sleep, so got up.

Brat-2 was awake and propped up against pillows on the floor. I curled up beside him and let him stroke my fur. Very quickly I realized that fleas were crawling all over his white baby-grow. That explains where my fleas came from. We lay together for a while, both scratching furiously.

4:20 PM: Helped with the kittens. I don't know why there are so many fleas around right now but after playing fights with Zucky for just a few minutes I discovered he had them too. Moments later his brothers and sisters were also being attacked by these vile vermin.

11:00 PM: Reluctantly I changed resolution number seven to 'I will not intentionally get fleas.'

It's a fact: a mother flea has so many children it's impossible for her to remember all their names.

28th July

(Another day of rest in honor of the Ancient Egyptian Cat Goddess Bast.)

The trees are full of happy birdsong. Baby birds demanding to be fed. Mother birds anxiously calling after fledglings that have wandered too far from the nest. Father birds working overtime to catch enough food to feed hungry families.

It's a fabulous time of year. It makes you think about the wonder of nature and the miracle of life. The best part of course is that the many baby birds that fall from the trees make really tasty snacks.

Spent all day pulling fleas out of my fur - I think for every one I catch another six jump onto me. My humans are all scratching too. Skirt has been putting white lotion on everyone. They all look like clowns - but no one is laughing.

It's a fact: a flea can jump a million times its own height. If cats could do that we could jump to the moon.

29th July

I was sitting under the rowan tree, minding my own business when a baby robin fell from the tree and landed on my head. He jumped off, sat in front of me and stared into my eyes.

"I can fly," he tweeted, ". . . well almost."

As I sat deciding whether to eat him immediately or keep him for later he chirped, "I'm Bobin, will you be my friend?"

"I can't," I said.

"Why?" he said.

"Because," I said.

"Why?" he said.

"Because I'm a cat," I said.

"Why?" he said.

"Because nature made me that way," I said.

"Why?" he said.

"Because nature decides everything about all the animals," I said.

"Why?" he said.

This went on for ages until, in desperation, I agreed to be his friend,

"I'm hungry," he said.

I ignored him.

"Food!" he insisted.

I ignored him.

"Food!" he demanded.

I ignored him.

"Food!" he pleaded, with a chirp so piercing it made my brain go numb.

I went to look for food.

Luckily I found a huge worm. I chopped it into pieces and popped them into his beak.

He sat looking quite happy for about four seconds then shrieked, "Food!!"

I decided I'd better find his parents and began searching the garden. I looked everywhere. I tried behind the shed and the greenhouse. I looked in every tree. I even sneaked into neighboring gardens but his parents were nowhere to be seen. At last I thought I'd better go back to guard the poor little thing. When I got to the rowan tree he was sitting on a branch with his mummy.

Seeing me coming he said, "Cat is my friend."

"He can't be your friend," said his mummy.

"Why?" he asked.

"Because I say so," said his mummy.

"Okay," he said.

30th July

Spent today scratching.

31st July
St. Ouch's Day - Patron Saint of Fleas

10:06 AM: Trousers and Skirt have gone mad. They are going from room to room with cans, spraying everything. They're spraying curtains and carpets and chairs and cushions - in fact everything that doesn't move. Just in case they decide to spray everything that does move, I'm getting out of here.

6:00 PM: Spent the day lying under the rowan tree enjoying the warmth of the sun. Bobin flew onto the tree and chirped, "You're not my friend."

"Why?" I asked

"Why why?" he asked.

He looked puzzled and flew away.

Fortunately my humans have stopped being mad but to be safe I have sneaked into the house and I'm hiding under the bed. My whole body is swollen and sore from flea bites. I think someone has opened a restaurant in my fur.

11:00 PM: My humans found me and sprayed me with that awful stuff. I smell so bad I won't be able to go out in public for a month.

1st August
(Lammas Day - first day of the catnip harvest.)

8:00 AM: Have just thoroughly checked my fur - all the fleas have fled. The awful smell from that spray has chased them away.

9:00 AM: An ancient old flea has just staggered out from under my bed coughing and spluttering. He said he was from the International Flea Institute for Biological Research which has operated from under the bed for the last five years. Apparently they had just discovered the formula for a serum that would allow all Creaturekind to live free from disease. He said that he was the only survivor of the Nuclear-Flea-Spray-Attack and as he had just minutes to live he must pass the formula on to me. He was most insistent that I let everyone know about the formula and said the future of the World was in my hands. It's very complicated so I must remember to write it in my diary later today. But now I must sleep - I'll need all my energy for tonight's Lammas Party.

2nd August

What a night!! The party was dead brilliant - there were hundreds of cats there. Snowball and I danced non stop through the night. I think she must have had too much catnip for she was a bit tipsy and wanted to sing all the time.

At dawn we sat on the top of Bluebell Hill and watched the sunrise over the oil refinery on the distant horizon. The rays, deflected by the smoke from the stacks, created the most beautiful spectrum of oily reds and sooty grays I have ever seen.

We kissed.

Snowball whispered, "I love you."

I was so shocked I was nearly dumbstruck. I mumbled, "I glug goo too." But she knew what I meant.

I am the happiest cat in the world!!

3rd August

As I rested under the rowan tree, Bobin landed on a branch above me. "Fly up and sit with me," he said.

"I can't," I replied.

"Why?"

"Because cats can't fly."

"Why?"

"Because we're not birds."

"Why?"

"Because nature wanted some creatures to live in the trees and some to live on the ground"

"Why?"

It suddenly occurred to me that perhaps the only reason that cats can't fly is because no one has ever bothered trying. Maybe I could be the first cat to fly. I could soar above the trees, swoop across mountains, and even fly to the moon. I sat up on my hind legs and flapped my front paws. I didn't move off the ground.

"Faster!" cried Bobin.

I flapped faster.

"Faster!"

I flapped even faster.

"Faster!!"

"Look at stupid Adrian trying to fly," came the irritating gruff voice of Brutus from across the fence.

I was too embarrassed to reply. I simply began washing my face as if that's what I had intended doing all along.

"Don't talk to Adrian like that," said Bobin.

"What are you going to do about it, small fry?" growled Brutus.

"I'll bash you," chirped Bobin.

"You and whose army?" yelped Brutus.

Bobin flew out of the tree, hovered a few feet above Brutus and pooed straight into his right eye. Shrieking with pain and humiliation, Brutus rushed indoors to tell his humans what had happened.

I like Bobin!

4th August

Finally persuaded Snowball to go with me to see the kittens. They showed their affection by climbing all over her. Snowball said they were very nice but as she had a headache she had to go home. On the way to her house she asked, "Have you been to the vet and had that operation that boys get?" When I told her I hadn't she said, "Pity."

Brutus is wearing a patch over his right eye. That will teach him to mess with me!

5th August

The Cosa Nostra gang met tonight. Killer had told us to bring along as much catnip as we could carry because there was going to be some 'action'. Don't know what he meant for we just played a betting game called Heads-or-Tails. Killer threw a mouse up in the air and we gambled on whether it would land on its head or its tail. I bet tails ever time - but it always landed on its head. The game ended when the mouse complained it had a sore head and Killer ate it. I had no catnip left anyway.

6th August

Went for a morning stroll in the woods. Heard a strange crying sound, a bit like Brat-2 on a bad day, so I went to investigate just in case he had escaped from the house. But it was a young fox. One of his legs was caught in a trap and he had been stuck there for three days without any food. I felt sorry for the poor thing, Kitsune is his name. I hurried to Old-Grey-Fur to get food. She gave me a chicken leg and I took it to Kitsune, without eating a single bite. I got Lucky to help me chew through the trap rope - it took us hours! Kitsune's leg must be broken for he was unable to walk. With our help, he managed to drag himself to the safety of a hollowed out tree. We'll take him more food tomorrow.

My teeth are aching!

7th August

11:00 AM: First thing this morning, I took some packets of Honey-Roast-Rabbit-Substitute-With-Additives-E205-and-E311-in-Mint-Sauce to Kitsune. He burst open the packets and scoffed the lot in two seconds.

He told me what had happened; he had been out with his mum and dad when they were spotted by a hunt. Before he could find cover, a pack of dogs were chasing after him. After running for miles he began to tire and the dogs closed in - he was sure he would be killed. Fortunately he came to some thorny briar bushes and was able to squeeze through them more easily than the dogs could. With a little distance between him and his assailants, he had a chance to escape. Ahead of him lay a stream. He outwitted his pursuers by running along the course of the stream causing the dogs to lose his scent. Feeling that he would soon be safe he headed for the cover of the woods but in his haste he didn't notice the trap.

11:11 PM: My humans had friends round for a barbeque. Trousers was surprised that the food disappeared so quickly. He had to drive to the shop to buy more. I now have enough meat to keep Kitsune going for days.

8th August

Snowball and I sat on the canal bank. I told her I love her without saying 'glug goo.' We kissed and she told me again that she loves me. We are so much in love, we didn't even bother when a man threw an old bike into the water and soaked us.

Kitsune is still in great pain.

9th August

Trousers painted my bedroom door. Naturally he didn't bother to tell me. I only found out when I head-butted it open. The white streak on my head makes me look like a punk.

Killer is taking us somewhere special tonight. It's a bit of a mystery. How exciting.

10th August

Last night Killer, Snowball, Lucky and I met at the park. Killer said we were going to spend the night at a haunted graveyard. I didn't like the sound of that one little bit but I didn't want to let Snowball think I was afraid.

We sat beside a tombstone, in the middle of the graveyard. No one spoke. It was dark and spooky. I quaked uncontrollably but I don't think anyone noticed. Just after the church bell struck midnight we spotted a ghostly cat shape creeping slowly towards us. I was terrified - so terrified that I couldn't even run away. But as the ghost got closer it tripped over a rock and swore angrily. It was only Satan with a tea towel over his head. Killer and Snowball were in hysterics laughing. I had just begun telling them that it was a mean trick to play, when they shrieked and everyone ran away, leaving me all alone. I turned round to discover another one of Killer's friends dressed as a ghost. His body was transparent and surrounded by a green, luminous glow - a brilliant costume I thought.

"Booooo," he said.

"Very funny," I replied.

"Booooo," he shrieked in his spookiest voice.

"Go away," I said, irritably.

"Are you not afraid of the dead?" he asked in a thin eerie voice.

"There's no such thing as ghosts," I replied.

"Yes there is," he said.

"No," I declared, "they're just tricks of the imaginations."

"Are you sure?" he asked, in a concerned voice.

"Absolutely," I insisted.

"Are you completely positive?"

"Definitely!"

With an unearthly wail, he vanished. What brilliant acting.

11th August

11:00 AM: Kitsune is getting weaker. I had to force him to eat a nutritional hamburger. I'm very worried about him.

7:00 PM: Brat sat me in the basket of his tricycle and we went round and round and round and round the garden. I'm still feeling giddy!

12th August

Told Snowball about Kitsune. She said, "Foxes are cruel and sly - as soon as he's better he'll eat you."

I don't think he would do that - but I'd best be careful. Kitsune is still very weak so, at least for now, I'm in no real danger.

13th August

The Cosa Nostra gang broke into the Duck and Sporran Pub tonight. When all the humans had left we crawled in through a little window at the back. Capo had broken in before and knew the layout. He led us through a maze of corridors into the lounge bar. Excitedly, Scarface leapt onto the counter and knocked over a bottle marked 'Balvenie Single Barrel Malt Whisky'. It smashed open and a sweet smelling amber liquid spread across the floor.

"Bottoms Up," cried Capo.

Everyone began lapping up the liquid. I took a sip - it was vile. The others seemed to be enjoying it so I tried another sip - that one wasn't so bad. I tried another. By the tenth sip, I thought that this was the best tasting drink in the whole wide world. We broke open another couple of bottles. I suddenly realized I loved the whole gang immensely and told them so. By now I was feeling uncontrollably happy and joined the others in a few songs. Strangely there seemed to be two Capos and two Satans, and two Scarfaces, and two Snapbones, and two Rosepetals. It just wasn't fair - they were all drinking twice as much as me!

Unfortunately, the pub owner must have heard our singing for he came rushing through the door looking very angry and fierce. For some reason we were unable to move in straight lines and were powerless to do anything as he threw us unceremoniously out onto the street.

It took me ages to stagger home - especially as I had to stop and tell every mouse I saw that they were unique, wonderful creatures.

14th August

My head aches!!
Brat-2 is crying.
Brat is shouting.
Trousers is hammering.
Skirt is making washing machine noises.
The racket is unbearable even though I'm curled up under my worry blanket in the shed.

15th August
(On this day in 2004 the exclusive cat restaurant, Meow Mix Café, opened on Fifth Avenue, New York.)

Lucky and I went fishing like wild cats. We chose a suitable spot on Cannies Burn and stood stock still on the bank. After a few minutes I spotted a fish and dived at it - but it darted away like a streak of underwater lightning. Lucky tried next but he was useless - even the fish laughed at him. Over the next three hours, we dived at fish after fish but all we caught were two pebbles and an old plastic bag. Cold, wet and hungry, we gave up. On the way home we raided the bins at the Uncanned-Fish-Shop. It's much easier catching fish from bins than from rivers. We took two fish to Kitsune and shared a third.

I wonder why Wild Cats don't just get their food from fish shop bins!!

16th August

It's official!!
Snowball and I have declared our eternal, undying love. Today we scratched each other's name onto a tree in the park. Now there is a clear

sign of our love for everyone to see.

Took Kitsune four packets of Cheap-Cut-Pork-Scraps-Marinated-in-a-Genetically-Modified-Lemon-Mousse - he barely touched them.

I think my humans are becoming suspicious - overheard Trousers say, "That darn cat's eating too much - he looks like a pregnant melon."

17th August

9:00 AM: Had a BRILLIANT idea!! I'm going to set up a rock band and become dead famous.

I will play drums. Lucky will be lead singer. My friends, Mungo and Gerry, the Siamese twins will be backing vocals.

Lucky suggested calling the band Queen, but after the incident with the letter I would not give her the free publicity. After a long debate we decided on the name The Doors.

4:08 PM: When Snowball heard about the band she couldn't decide whether she wanted to be in or out of The Doors. After much deliberation she is in. She is our new lead singer. Lucky is in the backing group.

10:30 PM: I am worried about Kitsune - he looks very weak.

18th August

Super day.

My humans gave me loads of presents; two purple mice containing catnip, a red-plastic-ball-with-a-bell-inside that makes a great noise when you roll it, and a squeaky-rubber-thing that goes, 'whheeeeeee' when you bite it.

Played ball with Brat all morning. We chased the ball up and down the garden until I fell asleep. When I awoke my humans brought me a huge cream cake with a candle on top and sang a song called 'Happy Birthday to You.'

Even Trousers was nice to me today. Not sure why.

19th August

Bobin landed at my feet, as I rested under the rose bushes.

"Why?" he asked.

"Why what?"

"Why are we here?" he asked probingly.

I searched through my memory bank for all the things I'd heard on analytical psychology theories of existence. I recalled the ideas of Cat Gustav Jung and Rene Des Cates. I tried to explain in the simplest way I could, "We exist because we are conscious of our own being - Cogito, ergo sum. And because our minds exist, our bodies must also exist for they house our minds. Thus, through our conscious minds we have an earthly presence - we are here because our minds tell us that we are here."

"Ohhh, that's strange," replied Bobin pensively. "You normally sit under the sycamore."

Before I could explain my philosophical theories further he was called back to the nest.

"You're my friend," he said, as he flew away. "But don't tell my mummy."

20th August

Killer, Satan, Scarface, Snapbone, and Rosepetal joined The Doors (it was Snowball's idea). Killer is drummer. I am now part of the backing vocals.

We held our first practice in the alley. Killer sat on the bins and used them as drums. The rest of us perched along the wall in a line. Must admit we were pretty good for a first attempt (though I'm definitely a better drummer than Killer).

Our best song is unquestionably Honky Cat, though Killer kept hitting the bin at the wrong time, Rosepetal got the words mixed up and Satan was consistently out of tune.

Honky Cat by Elton Marigold-John

You better get back honky cat

Living in the city ain't where it's at

It's like trying to find catnip in a mouse trap

It's like trying to drink milk from a water tap.

Some of the neighbors showed their appreciation by throwing old shoes at us. We ended our performance when the man from 48 set his Rottweiler on us.

For our next practice I need to learn the lyrics of the Cat Steven's song Moonshadow. It's rather a scary song - if I were being followed by a moonshadow I'd run like hell.

Moonshadow

Oh, I'm bein' followed by a moonshadow,

moonshadow, moonshadow

Leapin and hoppin' on a moonshadow,

moonshadow, moonshadow

And if I ever lose my paws, lose my bed, lose my litter tray,

Oh if I ever lose my paws, oh if I ever lose my paws,

I won't have to scratch wallpaper no more.

And if I ever lose my voice, if my purrs all run dry,

Yes if I ever lose my voice, oh if I ever lose my voice

I won't have to meow no more.

21st August

6:00 PM: Two men arrived in a white van and put a huge litter tray in my back garden. They filled it with heaps of lovely, clean sand. Another present from my humans. At times they are very kind and show almost catlike qualities. They must realize that it's not always comfortable doing my business amongst the bushes. Thank you humans. Brat was so excited with my litter tray that he jumped about in the sand for ages.

11:30 PM: I sat at the window watching all the cars driving along the street. It occurred to me that not one was being driven by a cat! Why don't they make cat cars? It would save us an awful lot of walking.

I used my new litter tray twelve times today (even though I only needed to go seven times) - it's fantastic!

22nd August

Brat was playing in my new litter tray this morning - humans are so very unhygienic!!

When I saw Kitsune today, I thought he was dead. He had a fearsome fever and was too weak to even move.

I rushed round to Snowball's and pleaded for help.

"Help save a fox!" she exclaimed, "Do I look like the International Red Cross?"

"But you must help - he's dying," I begged.

"The only good fox is a dead fox," she sneered. "When it dies, bring me its tail - I need a new cushion."

For someone who's so tender and caring she can be very heartless at times. It looks like it's up to Lucky and me to take care of Kitsune.

23rd August
(500th anniversary of the litter tray being invented.)

9:00 AM: Spent all last night with Kitsune - snuggled up against him to make sure he didn't get cold. His breathing is now very shallow and he just lies motionless.

4:10 PM: Lucky, Suffragette and the kittens arrived to see if they could help. It was the kittens' first outing and they were all carrying little bits of food for Kitsune - all except Zucky who had accidentally eaten his. The kittens were all on their best behavior and kept very quiet. We managed to get Kitsune to eat a little but he seems to have lost the will to live.

11:00 PM: There was a cat of 'no fixed abode' searching for scraps in the alley bins. As there wasn't much food to be found, I told her to try number 55 - the humans there seem determined to waste the Earth's resources, their bin is always full of perfectly good food. Personally, I'm a keen recycler - it's against my principles to let any food go to waste. The cat's name is Gypsy. She is very down to earth - possibly too down too earth - I don't think she's cleaned herself for weeks!!

24th August

11:50 AM: Met Gypsy again this morning. She had slept rough in the alley and was looking even more disheveled than yesterday. But when I told her about Kitsune, she immediately offered to help.

When we got to the woods, she took one look at him and said he had blood poisoning and would die in a few days if he didn't get medicine. She said that if we can get him some cotton thistle leaves quickly it might help. But it only grows on the shores Loch Lomond - and that's twenty-five miles away.

Lucky and Suffragette have offered to look after Kitsune while Gypsy and I go for the thistles.

25th August

11:35 PM: I'm exhausted!!

We set out for Loch Lomond yesterday afternoon. Gypsy is a very fast walker and I struggled to keep up. We got there at midnight but, as there was very little moonlight, it was too dark and dangerous to search for the thistles. We sat on the banks of the loch and talked and talked and talked. Gypsy told me all about her life. When she was a kitten she had lived with humans - but they were very cruel so she ran away from home. Ever since then she has been on the move, never settling in one place for more than a few weeks and never having friends. She's absolutely fascinating and has so many exciting tales to tell. I told her all about myself but didn't mention being part of a gang - somehow I find that side of my life a little embarrassing.

Before we realized it, the sun was rising over the loch and it was light enough to look for the thistles. I wish the night could have lasted much longer.

The thistles grow tall and were easy to find. Getting to them was the difficult bit for they were growing in the middle of marshland. We had to wade, tail deep, in sickly, slimy mud. It was disgusting.

The leaves were too high to reach, so we had to cut a plant down. As I chewed my way through the thorny stem, I felt as if my tongue was being attached by an army of fleas. Eventually, we felled a massive thistle and stripped off as many leaves as we could carry. With our mouths full we couldn't talk on the way home, which was a great pity for there was nothing I would have liked better.

When we got back, Kitsune was looking dreadful. Gypsy persuaded him to eat a couple of leaves - she will look after him while I get some sleep.

26th August

Gypsy and I spend the day looking after Kitsune - which was great for it gave us a lot of time to talk.

He ate four thistle leaves and by evening even managed a little food. His strength is slowly returning.

What a life Gypsy has led - she has been everywhere! Once she stowed away on a ferry to France and walked to Paris. She said it's a marvelous city and she loved sitting on the Champs Elysées just watching all the fashionable cats go by. Last year she spent several weeks in London. She told me that she slept on the embankment of the River Thames. There are hundreds of cats sleeping rough there but, unlike Gypsy, most of them would rather live in a comfortable home. Gypsy said it was very sad.

I asked her if she saw the Queen. She said that once, while dining from the bins at Buckingham Palace, (apparently the Queen lives there and not at Crystal Palace) an elderly lady wearing a crown shouted angrily at her from a very grand balcony, "One must not eat from the royal bins my dear." Minutes later, the royal corgis, turned up and growled regally at Gypsy in an attempt to chase her away - but they were so overweight she didn't even need to run. I said that setting her dogs on a defenseless cat sounded typical of what the Queen would do. Gypsy agreed and said, "Well what else would you expect from someone who prefers the company of dogs to cats?"

I told Gypsy a lot about myself. When I said that I am planning to become famous she said, "Why do you want to be famous?" I had to think hard for a while for I'd never really thought about it before.

"Just because," I replied, hoping that this summed up all my feelings and aspirations.

"Being happy in life is what's important," she said. "Fame and fortune mean nothing if you are miserable."

Then she asked me if I was happy.

"Of course I'm happy . . ." I replied immediately. I thought of my life;

a good home, Lucky and Killer as friends, being an important member of the Cosa Nostra gang, my wonderful girlfriend Snowball. " . . . sometimes." I added.

Gypsy is so interesting. Apart from wanting to become famous we have so much in common. We share the same political views, we like doing similar things, she even shares my quirky weakness for slugs marinated in mature compost.

In the evening Lucky and Suffragette brought food for Kitsune and we all talked for an eternity. Lucky and Suffragette seem to like Gypsy as much as I do. I'm looking forward to introducing her to Snowball and Killer - I'm sure they'll love her too.

27th August

4:00 PM: Kitsune was strong enough to sit up and talk. He thanked us profusely for taking care of him. He seems gentle and good natured; I really don't think I'm in any danger of being killed.

11:20 PM: I caught a couple of large mice and shared them with Gypsy. She was delighted. We sat with Kitsune, listening to all the noises of the woods and watching the shadows of the trees lengthening as the sun fell lower in the sky. Gypsy is like no other cat I know. There's something special about her that I can't describe. (I guess its similar to liking cream. I know I enjoy eating cream but find eating wood disgusting - yet I don't know why I should like one but not the other.) Anyway I really do enjoy her company - she's so much fun to be with.

28th August

Didn't get a chance to see Kitsune or Gypsy today, Snowball came round first thing wanting to talk.

She said she is trying to decide whether to settle down with me or take up a career as a glamour model. If she takes up modeling she'd be so busy that we would seldom see each other. I told her I'd be devastated if that happened. This pleased her and she purred proudly.

I tried to tell her what has happened over the last few days with Kitsune and Gypsy but she was so preoccupied with thoughts of becoming a super model that I don't think she heard a single word. Eventually she said curtly, "What you do in your spare time is up to you, but when that silly fox bites one of your legs off don't expect me to nurse you back to health."

29th August

Did a bit of Brat training.

I was sitting in the kitchen staring at my bowl hoping that someone would get the message that I was famished. Before I knew what was happening, Brat grabbed me and threw me out the door. I scratched it until he opened it again.

"Addy stay in," I said.

Giggling, "Addy Out" Brat threw me out again.

Once more I scratched and was let in.

"It's raining," I said forcefully, "Addy stay in!"

But even though I tried to run away I found myself on the wrong side of the door again.

"Let me in stupid," I meowed.

He did - but the moment I got in he threw me out again. This happened another six times until eventually I gave up and took refuge in the shed.

So now that he's got the hang of, "Addy out," I must teach him, "Addy In".

Kitsune has finished all the thistle leaves. Gypsy says he's getting better and doesn't need any more. Pity really, I wouldn't mind making the journey to Loch Lomond with Gypsy again.

30th August

We had another band practice this evening - what a shambles!

The drums were binging instead of bonging. I was the only one who knew the words. Satan and Scarface, didn't sing a note in tune. Rosepetal was worst of all. He sang;

"Oh, I'm being swallowed by a baboon's shadow, baboon's shadow, baboon's shadow.

Beepin' and sloppin' on a moonbuggy, moonbuggy, moonbuggy."

I'm too modest to write the rest!

Killer said we were brilliant and announced that we are to perform our first live gig next week. This is a total disaster. We must be the worst band since Simonese and Purrfunkel performed to an audience of one behind the toilets in New York's Central Park.

31st August

Lucky's parrot is infuriating. She still believes that she's a pirate and is now threatening to pressgang us into serving on her ship, the Jolly Roger. It's impossible to have a conversation with Lucky if Polly is any-where nearby. With her 'ahoy matey' and 'aarrrr Addy me lad' she's driving me crazy. But worse of all, she keeps making cheeky comments. Here are just a couple of the politer ones:

"Shiver me timbers, ye scurvy dog's will dance ze hempen jig for yer bilge." (Which means, "Good gosh, you wicked pirates will certainly hang for your foolish talk.")

"Ahoy, me mateys get me some grub and grog or ye shall get ten lashes o' ze cat o'nine tails." (Which means, "Hail, fellow sailors, I would be obliged if you could get me some fine food and alcoholic beverage - if you fail in this task the consequence is that you will be given a good hard flogging.")

1st September

1:00 PM: I am excited, worried and terrified. The Cosa Nostra gang will raid the Uncanned-Fish-Shop tonight. Killer has planned everything down to the minutest detail. He has left nothing to chance. We meet at 8:00 PM: - at 8:07 PM: precisely we will be dining on the best fresh salmon.

9:07 PM: The raid didn't go quite as planned - here's what happened:

8:00 PM: We all met in the alley behind the Uncanned-Fish-Shop. All except Satan. His human had fallen asleep and Satan had to do a lot of arm scratching before he managed to get himself thrown out of the house. (Humans are so unreliable.)

8:21 PM: Rosepetal began climbing up the drainpipe. His job was to break in through a skylight window and the rest of us were to follow.

8:25 PM: Rosepetal reached the roof and began crawling up the slope. He got about half way then began slipping down again. He desperately tried to cling on but the roof was too slippery. At the last moment he managed to grab hold of the gutter.

8:27 PM: Rosepetal held on desperately with just one claw as we devised a rescue plan.

8:29 PM: Rosepetal lost his grip and began his descent from the rooftop.

8:29 ½ PM: Rosepetal landed, head first, on the ground (disproving Newton's Law of Gravity - though maybe gravity was switched off at the time). Luckily, as he fell, he spotted a small ventilation hole just above the bins.

8:31 PM: We began scrambling in through the ventilation hole.

8:37 PM: Finally we had made it - we were all inside. Success. Or so we thought.

8:39 PM: We sat on the counter arguing over which slices of salmon to steal.

8:41 PM: The alarm went off.

8:41 ¼ PM: I panicked - I didn't want to do another stint in Cattery Prison.

8:41 ½ PM: We all tried to get out through the ventilation hole at the same time.

8:42 PM: Everyone began hitting everyone else.

8:43 PM: In the scratching, punching, and turmoil, I escaped through the hole.

8:49 PM: Everyone else got out.

8:50 PM: Police sirens were heard from every direction.

8:52 PM: Police rushed past us and smashed the shop door down.

8:52 ½ PM: We all ran for our homes.

That was a very narrow escape. I wonder why the police didn't suspect us of the robbery? I guess we all look so cute and innocent. It was a disappointing raid. We didn't get a single salmon - but at least we didn't get arrested.

Well as the great poet, Rabbie McTabby once said, "The best laid schemes o' mice an' cats gang aft a-gley" - which means, "The more Killer plans the more likely I am to end up in prison."

2nd September
(5000 years since catkind domesticated the human.)

8:40 AM: Brat was up early and dressed in nice new clothes. Today is his first day at something called Nursery-School. He's having a crying tantrum because he doesn't want to go.

2:10 PM: Brat is home again. He's having a crying tantrum because he wants to be back at the Nursery-School.

Nursery-Schools must be to humans what doors are to cats - when they're in they want to be out and when they're out they want to be in.

3rd September

*(Yet another day of rest in honor of the Ancient
Egyptian Cat Goddess Bast.)*

11:55 AM: As Snowball and I sat under the sycamore tree enjoying the sunshine, Bobin landed on a branch above us.

"Why are there two cats?"

"Because this is my friend Snowball."

"Why?"

"Because I like her."

"Why?"

"Because she's beautiful, caring, loving and kind."

"Why?"

"Go away you stupid bird," hollered Snowball.

"Why?"

"Because I'll rip your wings off if you don't!"

"Snowball," chirped Bobin sadly as he flew away, "you're not my friend."

I tried again to tell Snowball about Gypsy, for I'd like us all to be friends. But I think Snowball has a severe hearing difficulty for she only ever hears things about herself.

For exercise we strolled over to the apple tree and settled down there. "I've made an important decision," said Snowball earnestly.

"What's that?" I enquired.

"I've decided to sacrifice my career as a top model, for you" she replied, "and anyway I get sick traveling so I couldn't possibly tour the country."

I was absolutely thrilled.

"You won't regret it," I promised. "I would do anything for you."

"I know you would," she said, smiling. "That's what I like about you."

We spent the rest of the morning curled up together - life is bliss.

3:20 PM: With Brat at Nursery-School the garden seemed too quiet this morning. When he returned in the afternoon it seemed too noisy.

4th September

The kittens are two months old today. How they have grown. Soon they'll be looking for humans of their own. Suffragette is already worrying that they will end up with cruel cat-o-pathic humans who will torture them just for fun. Lucky and I have told her a million times that everything will work out - but still she frets.

Ducky was playing butterfly-chase in the garden while her brothers and sisters slept under the rose bushes. Four magpies suddenly appeared from nowhere and dive-bombed her. Suffragette must have a sixth sense, for although she was sound asleep beside us, she immediately charged across the garden to defend her daughter. Before Lucky or I could do anything, Suffragette leapt into the air and swiped two of the magpies - causing them to crash land. Then, with the grace and elegance of a lioness felling a gazelle, she lashed out at a third, ripping out several of its wing feathers. In embarrassment and fright, the magpies flew off as quickly as they could.

I was incredibly impressed by Suffragette's bravery and strength but Ducky hissed, "I could have dealt with them myself. Why do you always have to interfere in everything?"

Later we taught the kittens a nursery rhyme to remind them that magpies are deadly dangerous.

Magpie Menace

One for sorrow, two for pain,
Three for torture, four dine on your brain,
Five make you yelp, six make you cry,

Seven just for fun peck out your eye.
Eight for Satan, nine for Hell,
And ten do things too horrid to tell.

5th September

8:00 PM: For amusement, Lucky and I told Polly we'd found her ship the Jolly Roger. She was very excited and shouted things like 'pieces of eight' and 'splice the main brace', as she followed us to the canal.
"There it is," I cried, pointing to a wobbly raft made from old bits of wood.
Polly inspected it thoroughly.
"Aaarrrrr me mateys," she squawked, "all ship shape and Bristol Fashion. Climb aboard me hearties. We set sail for the Spanish Main."
With Lucky and I rowing we hit the high seas. Polly steered us carefully between invisible islands and hidden rocks (though I think Polly believed them to be real).
Under our captain's command we scuppered an old can and two bottles that were floating on the canal, and keelhauled their captains. Polly claimed these 'ships' and all their contents as the property of Pirate Polly. We all had a jolly good time and, had the ships been real, we would have been splendid pirates.
When we got back to Lucky's house, Polly showed us a secret map with a big red cross on it.
"Thar be treasure buried thar," she shrieked. "When ze wind blows from ze North West - ye shall help me find me booty and I'll reward ye with a handful of doubloons."
That parrot is utterly mad!!
11:00 PM: Found a huge steak in number 55's bin. It provided Kitsune, Gypsy and me with an excellent feast. Gypsy is doing a great job of looking after Kitsune and his leg is mending nicely. I told them about Polly and the pirate ship and we all had a great laugh.

6th September

Killer, Snowball and I met at the canal bridge. It was raining so we found a sheltered spot amongst the trees where we could talk. This seemed like the perfect time to mention Gypsy and tell them I'd like her to join our group. Even though I'd told Snowball everything I know about Gypsy, she asked some pretty dumb questions; "Is she a pedigree?", "Does she come from a good family?", "Does she wear expensive collars?"

I explained that Gypsy is a plain, down to earth type of cat who is not interested in material possessions but has a heart of gold.

Killer interrupted and said forcefully, "I hate strays. They all have fleas and worms and they carry infectious diseases that kill you if you get too close."

I tried to defend Gypsy saying that she knows all about herbal medicines and had cured Kitsune but my protests fell on deaf ears. Even though they have never met Gypsy neither Killer nor Snowball is willing to let her be part of our group.

I feel very sad. I can't remember ever feeling this miserable. I think I'll go and scratch Trousers!

7th September

5:00 AM: Woke up starving. Scratched on the bedroom door to let Skirt know I was hungry. She got up slowly, took ages putting on her dressing gown, and then had the cheek to go to the bathroom before serving me. Sometimes she stretches my patience!

6:00 PM: Went to see Suffragette and the kittens. I was greeted with a chorus of "We're going to your wedding. We're going to your wedding." from the kittens. They were so excited they jumped all over me and Suffragette had to pull them all off.

"Wedding?" I said in surprise, "What wedding?"

According to Suffragette, who heard it from Lucky, who heard it from Mungo, who heard it from the dog that lives next door to him, I am to be married to Snowball on the 2nd of November.

I rushed round to see Snowball - she confirmed it.

9:00 PM: Thought I should tell Gypsy and Kitsune about my forthcoming wedding, but they already knew. Gypsy and I took a walk. It was still raining but that didn't seem to matter. I told her a little about my future wife. She congratulated me and said I was very lucky to have found my perfect soulmate.

I am the happiest cat in the world - I think.

8th September

5:12 AM: Can't sleep for worrying. The band plays its first live gig today. We perform at a fairly prestigious location - the bins at the end of the Lane. Killer has invited just about every cat in town. This is it! My big opportunity! My big opportunity to look completely stupid in front of every cat I know!

6:25 PM: It was much worse than I could ever have nightmared. Dozens of my friends were in the audience. Killer introduced each member of the band then we kicked off with 'I Can't Get No Catisfaction'. Everyone, except me, was out of tune. No one even knew the words. We were horrific - talk about a cats' choir!! The audience began to titter and there were even a few hisses. Then a young impetuous cat, called Felix shouted out, "You are fishbones - total fishbones!"

Killer thumped the drums in anger and we all stopped singing. Rosepetal and Satan jumped into the audience and roughed Felix up. Our concert continued as if nothing had happened - except we now played to rapturous applause.

After the concert I walked Snowball home. She was delighted with the performance and thrilled at the standing ovation we received. I'm not sure whether she didn't realize we were 'fishbones' or whether she just doesn't care.

9th September

Spent today with Kitsune and Gypsy. Kitsune's leg was strong enough to take a short walk. He limps badly but Gypsy assured him that it will soon be as good as new.

I enjoy being with them. We can talk about politics, philosophy, food or just nothing in particular. I feel so at ease when I'm with Gypsy. She's so very attentive, kind, understanding, gentle, considerate, calm, sensitive and caring.

I wish Snowball was a little more like Gypsy.

10th September

9:00 AM: Trousers is all excited - a man delivered a new toy called a computer. Trousers started playing with it immediately. It looks like fun but he won't let me play.

10:00 AM: While Trousers was having a coffee, I tried the new toy. I discovered that by pressing a button marked 'DEL' I could make all the little characters disappear from the screen. Then by pressing buttons marked 'QWERTYU' I could make my own nice pattern on the screen. When trousers saw the screen he was jealous that my pattern was nicer than his.

11:00 AM: The computer is brilliant. There's a button marked 'EJECT' which causes a little tray to go out and in. It would appear to be a step to make it easier to climb onto the computer desk - great design feature but could do with being a bit sturdier for it couldn't even take my weight.

1:00 PM: While Trousers was having lunch I thought I would have a long time to play with the new toy but when I pressed the big button marked 'OFF' it stopped working. When Trousers returned he spent a lot a time saying his special words while studying a book called 'Fault Manual for Dummies.'

4:00 PM: Had another shot of the computer - there is a thing that looks like a mouse with a huge tail. Discovered that fighting the 'mouse' caused to the words 'Warning! You are about to erase the hard drive,' to appear on the screen. This was followed by a high pitched whirring noise that was so penetrating I was forced to make a dash for the shed.

5:00 PM: The man came back and took away the new toy.

10:00 PM: Trousers has been sulking all evening.

11th September

(The Battle of Stirling Bridge was fought on this day in 1297- the Scottish-Fold cat army thrashed the invading English Poodles.)

9:12 PM: Humans never fail to surprise me!!

I was taking a casual stroll through the gardens of Acorn Avenue, when I was pounced on from behind. To my shock and horror, it was the mass murderer from number 96. I was being kidnapped without my permission. He must be made of steel, for no amount of scratching and biting produced even a trickle of blood - just laughter at my attempts to get free.

As he carried me into his house, I had visions of all sorts of implements of torture; cat o' nine tails, whisker tuggers, tail stretchers, paw crushers . . .

To my great surprise, he sat me gently on the floor and produced a plate of medium-rare-sirloin-steak. I ate it quickly, just in case he would be offended and murder me. When I'd finished, he sat me on his lap and saying, "nice kitty," and "who's a good puss" stroked me very gently. I noticed for the first time, that as well as tattoos of snakes and lady humans he has dozens of cat tattoos all over his arms. I sat on his lap for an hour or so before making my excuses and leaving.

It appears that he is not a cat killer - in fact he seems to have an abnormal fondness for cats. I do hope he's not some kind of mad stalker!!

12th September

Gypsy makes Kitsune do exercises to make his leg strong again. Today I joined in; we did push ups, stretches, running on the spot and air punching. By the time we were finished, I was exhausted and had to take a nap. I don't know how Gypsy and Kitsune manage to do this ten times a day!

The man at number 96 put a large fish out on his doorstep when he saw me at the top of his garden. I shared this with Gypsy and Kitsune. As we ate I told them that Mr. 96 seems kind and gentle even though he is covered in tattoos. Gypsy said, "It just proves that you can't tell a book by its cover."

I replied, "And you can't tell the temperature of a central heating radiator by its color - often it's only after getting your nose burnt that you realize it's far too hot."

Gypsy looked bemused by this - but I expect she's never seen a central heating radiator.

In the evening Lucky and Suffragette brought the kittens to see Kitsune. We all played tig-tail for ages and had a huge amount of fun.

Later, when Lucky and I were alone, we sat on the bins and talked about life and everything. Lucky said something that is very stupid but, at the same time, remarkably sensible. He said, "Adrian, you are a very lucky cat. Very soon you will marry the most beautiful girl in town. Yet, it's only when you're with Gypsy that you seem to appreciate how lucky you are - most of the rest of the time you are miserable."

It was a strange thing to say and I wish I understood what it means - for I think that it's true.

13th September

We pulled off our most daring crime ever!

All members of the Cosa Nostra met at the mall at 10:00 AM precisely. Killer gave us our instructions;

Satan and Scarface were to cause a distraction while the rest of us pick-pocketed the unsuspecting shoppers. Killer would supervise from a vantage point beside the exit door. Satan and Scarface went into action, chasing each other in circles and howling at the top of their voices. It worked well, most shoppers stopped what they were doing, sat their shopping on the ground and watched the chase. The rest was easy!! Shoppers are so gullible!! We simply rummaged through their bags, taking anything of interest. We did this scam six times, at different points in the mall. I got a huge packet of honey-roast-ham, four packets of corned beef, a small pork steak and a rather colorful container marked, One-a-Day-Multivitamins-and-Minerals-with-Odourless-Garlic-Lutein-and-Iron. The others did well too. We gathered outside the shop to share out the loot. Killer gave each of use a packet of meat. He will safeguard the rest. We threw away the One-a-Day-Multivitamins-and-Minerals-with-Odourless-Garlic-Lutein-and-Iron as it looked rather unhealthy.

I took the Ultra-Low-Budget-Reconstituted-Spam, that I was allocated, to Kitsune. He is always very grateful when I take him food and promises that somehow he'll repay me when he's well again.

14th September

Spent today at Lucky's. Since our sail on the Jolly Roger we have become quite good friends with Polly. She told us a story of when she was shipwrecked on a tiny desert island. After her ship was attacked and scuppered, Polly, the only survivor, was washed up onto the beach. She was all alone. There was no human to bring her seed and nuts - no cuttlefish to keep her beak sharp. For months she had to struggle by on just coconuts, oranges, guava, peanuts, pineapples, mangoes, grapes and bananas. All this time she didn't see a living soul, apart from the seagulls that colonized the island - but their conversation was always about wind strength and the probability of rain so they didn't count. Just when Polly thought she'd go crazy with loneliness, she spotted footprints in the sand. Human footprints! She followed them to a little hut made from mud, leaves and branches. Inside was a young, fair haired car salesman. He had come to the island several years previously on a package tour but had missed the ship for home. The two became great friends. Polly called him Tuesday - for that was his name. Eventually after many daring adventures together, Polly was rescued by an illegal bird-trapper and taken to a back street pet shop in Edinburgh. It was from there that she came to her present home with Lucky.

15th September

Lucky and Suffragette are looking after Kitsune so that Gypsy can have a break.

I took her for a walk to the Council Dump. We watched the huge tipper trucks shovel rubbish into massive pyramid shaped piles. Gypsy said she loved the sound of the cans and bottles being crushed.

I said that each pile was like a little Everest - a monument to the joint achievement of catkind and humankind. Mountains of discard - each a testimony to the ingenuity of our civilization. We laughed and laughed as we watched the wind lift bits of litter from the heaps and scatter them across the organic farmland that surrounds the dump.

We found a container of six day old Sweet-and-Sour-Chicken. I said it was half empty, Gypsy said it was half full. She is such an optimist! The meal had matured nicely and we ate is slowly as we chatted. Gypsy said that she couldn't remember ever staying in one place for such a long time.

She said that she likes it here and is in no hurry to leave. I told her I would be delighted if she stayed around for a long, long time.

We took the scenic route home, along the canal. Just past the Sewage Works I spotted Snowball on the other banking a little way off. I called to her but, although she seemed to be looking straight at us, she hurried away in the opposite direction.

Today has been brilliant!

16th September

Brat-2 was playing on the carpet this morning and managed to crawl cat-style. Skirt got all excited and clapped her hands with glee. Brat-2 grinned happily, tried to clap his hands too, and fell with a thud onto the carpet. Having learned that he can't cat-crawl and clap at the same time, he managed to crawl several more times during the day.

It seems to me that evolution has advanced humankind to a new level and that the next generation will be able to crawl rather than walk on just two legs. Maybe one day they will also learn to meow.

17th September
(50th Anniversary of the Great Scratchpad Revolt - when the cats of Edinburgh rebelled against the introduction of tweed scratchpads.)

6:30 AM: Snowball arrived at my door. She insisted that I sign a prenuptial agreement. It read:

> *a) I will devote myself entirely, completely and*
>   *utterly to Snowball.*
> *b) I will never even look at another girl and will never have*

even a meaningless relationship with anyone else.

c) I will give Snowball an abundance of presents at very regular intervals.

d) I will become powerful and famous.

e) I will support Snowball in the comfort and style to which she intends becoming accustomed.

f) Should I meet an untimely death through gang warfare, retaliation, jealousy, acts of nature, food poisoning, etc etc I leave all my possessions to Snowball.

g) I will visit the vet for a boys-operation at my earliest convenience.

As I love and trust Snowball implicitly, I signed immediately. I asked if she would also be signing a prenuptial. Fortunately she had thought about that too and had already signed one. It read;

a) Providing Adrian remains faithful, loving, considerate, generous, becomes famous, and does not become too unattractive, I promise to remain reasonably faithful and moderately dedicated to him.

I am delighted that she's signed something that shows her intention to be faithful and dedicated to me. I think it says a lot about her commitment.

18th September

10:30 AM: Brat-2 is becoming quite proficient at cat crawling. Now we can play chasing games. Sometimes he chases me - sometimes I chase him. As I'm so much faster than he is, I often bump into his bottom causing him to do roly-polys across the floor. How we laugh!

9:10 PM: Took Kitsune a couple of packets of Fictitious-Turkey-(maximum 3.2%)-with-Animal-Entrails-and-Derivatives-plus-Cereals-Vegetable-Protien-Extracts-Minerals-and-Unpermitted-Colourants stolen from the cupboard. Kitsune insisted that Gypsy and I go for a walk saying that he would be fine on his own.

We walked through the park and sat by the pond. Eventually talk got round to the subject of my forthcoming marriage. Gypsy has very traditional views on marriage and kittens; believing a wife should be devoted to looking after her husband and should have lots of kittens.

"Snowball only wants a few kittens," I said, trying to hide my sorrow. "How few?" she asked.

"Approximately none," I admitted.

I could tell Gypsy was shocked but she said nothing - she never criticizes anyone.

"Have you ever thought about marriage?" I asked.

"I've never been in one place long enough to even make friends," she said.

"You must have friends," I said.

She thought for a moment and then said earnestly, "You are the only friend I've had since I was a kitten."

I purred. Inside I felt a strange warmth. I am delighted that Gypsy thinks of me as a friend - she is so different from any other cat I've ever met.

11:30 PM: Have been thinking about Snowball and Gypsy - there's such a huge difference between loving and liking someone!

19th September

5:00 AM: When I went out to do my business, Snowball was standing on the doorstep. Before I could even say, "Good morning my precious, darling sweetheart" she snapped, "Where were you yesterday?"

"With Kitsune," I replied defensively.

"You were with that hussy Gypsy," she hissed angrily.

"She may have been around when I was with Kitsune but to be honest I don't recall seeing her," I lied - not really knowing why.

"You are never to see her again," she said.

"Why?" I gasped.

"Because I say so," she replied.

Before I could utter a word of protest, she was gone.

I'm so confused - why does Snowball not want me to see Gypsy? Does she really believe what Killer says about catching deadly diseases from strays?

20th September

(On this day in 1767 Catgang Amouser Mozart wrote Symphony #42 for the Tinkly Bell.)

Trousers and Skirt have gone out. Wrinkly-Skirt is looking after Brat, Brat-2 and me.

She hasn't fed me, patted me, talked to me, groomed me, or even opened a door for me. In fact her only acknowledgement of my presence was hitting me with a newspaper whenever I went near Brat-2.

Although she obviously loves me, she often manages to give the impression of not actually liking me.

Lucky came round. I had another attempt at climbing a tree - but now, if I even touch the bark, the whole nightmare of having to be rescued by firemen floods my mind with fear. I have become an emotional wreck. Lucky says he knows someone, who knows someone, who knows someone, who knows a psychiatrist who can help me. He's going to arrange an appointment.

Lucky and I took some food, scavenged from the bins, to Kitsune and Gypsy. I thought it best not to stay with them for long for Snowball has a sixth sense that lets her know my every move.

21st September

Brat and I played chess - the intellectual sport. He's not very good - I had knocked all my pieces off the board before he had even knocked three down. Then we played pawn-football. I won by four scratches to one.

22nd September

Under protest I went to see Lucky's, friend's, friend's, friend's friend Professor Sigmund Dixie-Belle Fraud. Sigmund told me to lie comfortably and relax. Relax! How could I possibly relax! I was with a psychiatrist - you'd need to be crazy to be able to relax with a psychiatrist!

He held a feather in front of me and waved it slowly from side to side. The next thing I remember is having a dream; Gypsy had wings like an angel and was flying through the air, Snowball was flying too - in a SU-37 Terminator fighter plane and firing missiles at Gypsy.

Sigmund's soft voice cut through my dream, "You are a kitten once more. Look, see your mummy, see your brothers and sisters."

I suddenly felt incredibly hungry.

"Mummy, mummy," I said, "feed me."

"Get to the back of the queue, stupid," said my little brother Splat.

"Yeah, you were fed last week," said my big sister Jumbo.

"It's not easy looking after a family of twelve," said my mummy softly. "I mean I've got my career to keep up as well."

"Remember those halcyon days of childhood," interjected the distant voice of Professor Fraud, "when you didn't have a care in the world."

"Adrian," said my father sharply, "go and find straw to line the nest box."

"And bring back some juicy mice for your brothers and sisters," added mummy.

"I want a vole," said Susiecute.

"Get me cheese," demanded Cheddar. (He always was the strange one in the family.)

" . . . okay Adrian," came the professor's voice. "I'm bringing you back to the present, but you will retain all the happiness of your child-hood."

When I was out of the trance, I asked, "Did you find out what's wrong with me?"

"Yes . . .yes . . . it's more serious than I had expected," said the professor pensively. "You have an extreme Eodi-Puss complex. Through semi-conscious repression this has resulted in your developing severe thermal neurosis and parasitical hysteria. But, rather than accept the truth, you have transposed these conditions into a fear of trees."

"What can I do?" I asked desperately.

"While under hypnosis, I have told your inner consciousness that there is nothing to be afraid off - you are now completely cured."

"Thanks," I said gratefully.

"No problem." he replied. "Pay my receptionist twenty pieces of cat-nip and make weekly appointments to see me for the next four years."

As I walked away he added, "Your lucky number is forty-two but beware of the color yellow-ochre. I also foresee that you will find happi-ness where you least expect it and sadness where you most expect it."

23rd September

I found a new box in my bedroom. It's gold colored, hexagonal in shape and has a little label that reads, 'Verscratchy Couture Exclusive Designer Hats'.

I prized open the lid and was delighted to discover that Skirt had lined the inside with a soft blue material. She must love me a lot! For some rea-son known only to herself, she had attached plastic fruit and flowers to the lining material, but already I've managed to chew much of it off.

I squeezed in - a perfect fit. There is something mystical about boxes - I could sleep in one for days without tiring.

My fun was disturbed by Skirt coming into the room. She seemed upset and unceremoniously ejected me from my box. I expect that she was keeping it to give me on a special occasion and I've spoiled the surprise.

24th September

9:00 PM: Snowball and I met for lunch at her house. Her humans are very generous with food - pity it's vegetarian rubbish and completely inedible. I only ate it to please my darling Snowball.

"Our relationship is based on honesty and trust," she said, while chewing a mouthful of Genuine-Hay-Stubble-with-Thyme-Lemon-Ginseng-and-Salt-Free-Organic-Seaweed.

"Of course it is," I replied, "complete honesty and total trust."
"And you would never lie to me?" she said in a sort of interrogating way.
"Never," I concurred.

"Or do anything I didn't want you to do," she said, in a way that resembled getting electro-shock treatment to the brain.

"Never," I agreed.

"Have you been seeing that bitch Gypsy again?" she asked in an almost manic tone.

"No, of course not," I lied. I blushed bright red - but fortunately my thick fur hid my guilt.

"I wouldn't dare do anything to upset you," I added hastily.

I wanted to ask her why I shouldn't see Gypsy but feared I might upset her even further. But our relationship is based on honesty and trust just as she says, so I know she's only doing what's best for me. I resolved there and then, never to see Gypsy again. And anyway, now that Kitsune is getting stronger, there's no need for me to go anywhere near them.

11:57 PM: I wonder if Kitsune and Gypsy are still awake. I can't sleep.

25th September

8:00 AM: To celebrate my recovery from dendrophobia, Lucky and I are going on a chestnut hunt. We have wagered two mice on who can find the most chestnuts in twenty minutes.

1:08 PM: I have never been so embarrassed in all my life (apart from the time I had to be rescued by the fire brigade). Lucky and I went to the park and selected a suitable tree. With a 'ready' - 'steady' - 'go' we were off - or to be more precise Lucky was off up the tree. When my paws touched the bark my whole body turned to jelly. I quivered and shook with fear.

"Come on Tarzan," called a squirrel from a nearby tree. "Let's see you climb."

I sat at the foot of the tree grooming myself pretending that I didn't really want to climb.

"Are you a cat or a mouse?" called another squirrel.

I remained motionless - apart from shaking and quivering.

"Silly cat mouse . . . silly cat mouse," called a group of young squirrels.

I couldn't take any more. With my tail between my legs I slunk off in disgrace.

Lucky, of course, was very supportive. "That's two mice you owe me you pathetic cowardly-cat" he said, repeatedly.

11:00 PM: I hope Kitsune and Gypsy are okay. I miss them dreadfully.

26th September

Awoke from a restless sleep still worrying about Kitsune and Gypsy. Grabbed three packets of food and set out for the woods. My worries were unfounded for they were both well. Kitsune's leg will soon be back to full strength.

Gypsy suggested going for a walk but I was afraid Snowball would see us so I said I was tired. As we lay in the grass, I asked Gypsy if she would leave Bearsden when Kitsune was fully recovered. She said that she would probably stay a little longer. I suggested adopting a human for a few weeks but she doesn't want the commitment.

As the afternoon wore on, a chill wind blew through the trees and we curled up close to keep warm. I felt happy and content just resting close to Gypsy as we watched the leaves tumble from the trees. It was so peaceful and relaxing. It was with great reluctance that I headed home.

At the bridge I met Snowball. She immediately asked me what I had been doing. When I told her that I'd spent the whole day thinking about our wedding she smiled and gave me a big kiss.

27th September

Killer turned up at my house just as I was about to go for a sleep in the shed.

"I need your help," he said.

I felt very important! Killer needs my help!!

"I'd do anything to help you" I said.

"I know," he replied with a grin. He continued, "There have been complaints from lots of cats in the town about that friend of yours - that straggly stray thing."

"Do you mean Gypsy?" I asked in surprise.

"Yes, that's the name," he replied. "Apparently she's spreading diseases."

"She can't be," I exclaimed. "She's very healthy and quite clean."

"Well you can help me to help her," he said.

"Tomorrow evening at six, bring her to the bridge. If she's as healthy as you say she is I'll tell the complainers that they're wrong about her."

"Thanks," I said. "That's kind of you."

"Anything to help a friend of yours," he said. "But don't tell her about our conversation, just in case she gets scared."

Killer really does have a kind, gentle side.

28th September

11:12 AM: It's cold and windy outside. Winter is not far away. But I am sitting under the radiator feeling warm and smug. In just a few hours Killer will see what a nice respectable cat Gypsy is. Once he gives her his approval she'll be accepted into our group and we can all be friends. Snowball may even make her a bridesmaid at our wedding!!

Life is perfect . . . well almost perfect. Since Brat-2 learned to cat-crawl he finds it amusing to sneak up on me and pull my tail. I need to be on constant tug-alert. I do hope tails are not easily detachable.

11:59 PM: What a horrid, detestable, life shattering evening!! Here are the awful details.

Took a slice of fish (donated by Old-Grey-Fur) to Kitsune and Gypsy. After they had eaten, I asked Gypsy if she would like to go for a walk with me. She seemed somewhat surprised at this for it was raining mice-and-dogs but she agreed and we set off leaving Kitsune to have a rest.

As we got close to the bridge I saw that Killer was there as promised. "I'd like you to meet a good friend of mine," I said to Gypsy. "He's going to help you."

Killer looked formidably large towering over Gypsy. He looked her up and down in a condescending manner. "So you're the one that's causing all the trouble," he said sarcastically. "You look the type."

Gypsy looked at me and I saw panic in her eyes. I didn't know what was happening but I realized I'd done a foolish thing. Killer whistled and the Cosa Nostra gang appeared from the trees. I saw Snowball there too - peering out from behind a tree. The gang surrounded us.

"This is a respectable town," said Killer. "There's no room for flea ridden, scabby strays."

The others chanted things like, "take a hike fleabag", "we hate smelly strays", and "kill the witch".

Gypsy said nothing but her eyes accused me of betraying her.

Silently she walked off the bridge and along the canal bank.

After a few moments she turned and said sadly, "I thought the cats here were nice, but every single one of you is horrid." A tear rolled down her cheek as she continued, "I'm leaving this ghastly place and I'll never come back."

"Get her!" commanded Killer.

Terror-stricken I watched as the gang chased her along the canal, scratching and spitting at her until they disappeared into the distance.
I stood on the bridge feeling wretched and pathetic.

"You're better off without her," said Killer. "Trust me, I just did you a big favor."

I walked for hours in the pouring rain feeling miserable, dejected and confused. Perhaps Killer and Snowball are right. Perhaps it's better that Gypsy has gone. But right now it feels as if my whole world has ended.

29th September

3:00 PM: Early this morning I took food to Kitsune. He was very worried that Gypsy hadn't returned last night. I told him that she'd met an old friend and had to leave town in a hurry. I quickly left for home for I didn't want to have to answer any awkward questions.

Snowball was waiting for me. She was very cheerful and insisted that we go for a walk in the park. We did so, but my heart wasn't in it - I kept thinking about Gypsy. She had said I was her first friend - I have let her down badly! I expect I'll be her last friend.

8:20 PM: Trousers is in a very good mood today. Skirt had made him a cake with hundreds of candles on it. When they were all lit I was worried that the house would burn down. (Humans do such foolish things.)

Wrinkled-Skirt, Skirt and Brat sang the Happy-Birthday song and then Trousers blew out the candles. He blew them out eight times before they were all out. Skirt gave him a bottle marked 'Bruichladdich Single

Malt Rare Scotch Whisky.' He opened it and has been drinking the liquid ever since. It made him wobbly and caused him to become affectionate towards me. He kept picking me up to kiss me on my head - but the smell from his breath was so strong it almost made me wobbly too. I'm going to lie on the stairs to get out of his way - I much prefer when he's unaffectionate to me.

11:50 PM: We had a little accident! Trousers climbed the stairs to go to bed and didn't realize that I was sleeping near the top. He tripped and fell all the way back down. What a fuss he made. He lay on the carpet moaning and groaning like a Manx that had just discovered he has no tail.

A little later a car marked 'AMBULANCE' arrived at the door and took Trousers away. I hurt my tail in the accident but nobody cares.

30th September

9:00 AM: When I awoke, Trousers was sitting on my favorite chair. I asked him politely to feed me. He said something in those strange words and kicked me with his unplastered leg.

2:00 PM: I have come to the shed, wrapped myself up in my worry blanket, and will stay here until the world gets better.

1st October

Snowball and I sat on Bluebell Hill and chatted for much of the day. I told her I was upset about Gypsy being driven out of town. Snowball pretended that she knew nothing about it.

She said, "Adrian, Gypsy is just a stray. She's not worth getting upset about."

"But she is so kind and gentle," I replied.

"She is a cat of no importance," said Snowball forcefully, "no use to you or to me."

"But I feel guilty about what happened," I confessed.

"It was out of your hands Adrian - there was nothing you could do."

"Poor thing. She hasn't a friend in the world," I said sadly.

"Look Adrian," said Snowball, snuggling up to me. "It's a new month - Gypsy is a thing of the past. Forget her. We have more important things to think about."

Snowball quickly changed the subject. She talked at length about a wonderful collar she had spotted in a shop window. It's made from white satin and covered in a rainbow of jewels. She wants to wear it at our wedding and will be devastated if she can't get her paws on it.

2nd October

The kittens are all excited. Prospective new humans have been coming to the house. Suffragette has examined each one thoroughly and declared that none of them is good enough. Lucky told her that she's being over protective and she slapped his ear. The kittens are eager to be independent but it will be sad to see them leave home.

Trousers has taken up residence on my favorite chair again - he's been sitting on it all day. He does this every time he breaks a leg!!

3rd October

When he got back from Nursery-School, Brat and I went into the garden. There was a small injured mouse hobbling along the side of the shed. This seemed like the ideal opportunity to teach Brat the art of mousing. Being careful not to frighten the mouse away, I showed Brat where she was. The silly boy just stood and giggled at her. I demonstrated how to jump and stun; with a single leap I was on the little critter and thumped her on the head. Brat stopped giggling. I sat the mouse on the grass and allowed her time to come round again. Slowly, she got to her feet and saying a little prayer, "Hail Mother Mouse, full of mercy, protect me from evil cats . . ." began limping towards the shed.

"Get her!" I meowed, "Kill her!" but Brat stood still and looked confused.

With the mouse about to escape I took action; I pounced on her and knocked her head against the shed.

"That's how it's done," I meowed, and placed the dead mouse at Brat's feet.

Brat started crying and ran indoors. I don't know why he was so upset - even the brightest of kittens couldn't possibly learn everything in just one lesson.

Hucky is the first of the kittens to adopt a human. She left this morning for her new home. Suffragette was in a terrible state and couldn't stop crying. Really, I don't see what all the fuss is about - she's only moving next door.

4th October

On Killer's command, I met him at the park.

"I hear that trees frighten you," he said.

"None have ever intentionally frightened me," I said in their defense.

"They've never actually threatened me - in fact I don't recall any tree ever even speaking to me."

"What I mean," said Killer, in a very condescending voice, "is that you're such a scaredy-cat you can't climb trees."

"I'm not scared," I said, feeling deeply insulted by this accusation, "but I do have the tiniest little bit of a phobia . . ."

"I'll cure that," interrupted Killer, "for I don't allow cowards in my gang."

Before I could think of a witty reply that would show I'm not a coward without offending Killer, he unshackled his claws and thrust them in front of my nose. They are massive and sharpened to perfection - he must work out a lot! To show me how sharp they are he struck a passing bee - it fell at my feet in four pieces.

"If you're not at the top of that tree in sixty seconds," he said, pointing to a massive oak, "I'll skin your hide and use the fur to line my sleeping box."

He sounded serious. His big green eyes were fully dilated, making him look even more insane than usual. I moved towards the tree but I knew I couldn't possibly climb it.

With fully extended claws Killer lunged at me - I scrambled out of his way.

"Well done," he said, from below, "forty two seconds is a pretty good time. Now get down immediately, or I'll come up and throw you down"

Under Killer's supervision I climbed six trees today and have completely overcome my phobia.

When I thanked him for helping me, he said, "You've got to be cruel to have fun."

But of course he'd got his metaphors mixed up. He meant to say, "You've got to be cruel to be kind." He may be kind but he's not very smart.

5th October

My humans bought me two small fresh fish today (though Brat thinks they are his). To ensure that they stay fresh until I'm ready to eat them they have put them in a round bowl filled with water. My humans really are kind to me. Brat has called the fish, Tinky and Winky. They are most upset about this (their real names are Xin and Xout) for tinky and winky are very rude words in fish language.

I enjoy watching them swimming - it's like having my very own cat-television. I asked them why they kept swimming round and round the bowl. They told me that whenever they try swimming square and square they keep bumping their noses against the bowl. I'm not sure how long the fish will stay fresh in water but I'll save them until I'm really hungry.

Lucky and I have been taking it in turns to look after Kitsune. He almost caught a rabbit today so very soon he'll be able to fend for himself.

6th October

Zucky, Yucky and Rucky have adopted humans. They have found homes within easy walking distance of their mother and have promised to visit often. Suffragette is distraught and is refusing to come out of her sleeping box. Lucky is being very supportive and is constantly reassuring her that the kittens will be safe and happy. Lucky has a black eye and a badly scratched ear.

The Cosa Nostra gang met on High Street for a special-mission. So special that Killer was to carry out the raid himself (with our help of course). He carefully explained the plan and we made our way to a shop called, 'Amanda's Exotic Pet Shop'.

While Snapbone and Rosepetal guarded the entrance, Satan, Scarface, and I ran inside, found the budgerigars, and began thumping on their cages to cause a commotion. While Amanda tried to chase us away, Killer darted in, grabbed the target item and ran out again. The raid was all over in minutes and was a great success. I'd love to know what Killer stole.

7th October

6:00 PM: It was Skirt's turn for cake today. Trousers gave her a lot of brightly colored parcels. Most were very big and contained black cooking pots - Skirt didn't seem very pleased with these. The smallest parcel contained a little finger collar with a bright green stone on it - even though it was the smallest present, Skirt liked it best. Brat gave her a card he had made at Nursery-School. (but to be honest I could have done better myself). Brat-2 gave her nothing in particular but was sick all down her good dress.

I thought it only proper that I give her something too. I searched for ages for a mouse or small rat but as it was cold and wet I expect they are all wrapped up warm in their nests.

I was about to give up when I remembered the large spider that had recently taken up residence in the shed. He's almost the size of a mouse and his body is covered in a thick mass of hair. I carefully carried him into the house, jumped onto Skirt's lap and dropped my present onto her knee. Well, you would have thought I'd given her a dissected-cow-in-formaldehyde for she screamed and jumped so high she nearly hit the roof. How was I to know she has spider-phobia?

To try and make things better I swallowed the spider but that just made her scream even louder. There's no pleasing some humans!

11:58 PM: I am pleased to report that Skirt did not get drunk and fall down the stairs.

8th October

All the kittens have now got homes and all close to Suffragette. Mucky has adopted the man at number 96 Acorn Avenue and is very happy.

I went to see Snowball this morning. With great pride she showed me the collar she will wear at our wedding. It's made from white satin and covered in a rainbow of jewels. She looks absolutely fantastic wearing it. I will be very proud of her on our wedding day.

Our wedding plans are further advanced than I realized. The guest list has been created and arrangements made for us to spend our honeymoon at the cottage at Loch Lomond where Snowball's cousin lives.

When I said that I'd better let Lucky know his duties as best-cat, Snowball said irritably, "We couldn't possibly have Lucky as our best-cat."

"But he's my best friend," I said.

"He's a cat of no social standing," she replied, as if this explained everything.

"But I like him," I said.

"Don't be so selfish," she scolded. "It's important that everything is perfect for my wedding." She paused for a moment to brush her tail and then continued, "and anyway, Killer has already agreed to be best-cat."

"Killer!" I exclaimed, in shock, surprise, amazement and horror.

"Yes. Killer is the perfect best-cat," she said. "Once we're married I expect we'll be seeing a great deal of him."

Killer as best-cat! I suppose I should be honored but I feel sorry for Lucky. He will be so disappointed.

9th October

7:03 AM: Everything in my life is changing fast. There's so much happening. Soon I'll be a married cat with lots of responsibilities. I need time to think. I shall visit Old-Grey-Fur - I'll have peace to reflect and deliberate there.

11:49 PM: Old-Grey-Fur and I slept all day. I feel much better. Everything has cleared in my mind. I am now even more appreciative of Snowball's love and I am even more delighted that Killer is willing to help me become the cat that Snowball wants me to be. I feel happier than I have for days.

10th October

10:00 AM: Killer has called the gang together. He says that he has an old score to settle. Everyone has to meet in my garden at midday.

11:00 PM: When we met, Killer explained that he wanted revenge on Brutus for hurting him in the fight they had a few months ago. He said six brave cats would have no trouble with such a mangy little dog. He also promised that, once we duff him up, Brutus will never bother me again. Killer explained the tactics. We would attack in V formation, with the newest member, me, at the front.

Rosepetal and Scarface would be right behind me with Satan, Snapbone and Killer bringing up the rear.

We crept through the hedge at the back of the garden. In V formation we began our maneuver, edging slowly towards our victim. He didn't spot us until we were only a few meters away.

As Brutus jumped up growling, Killer shouted "Kill the sucker." We all ran forward but as we came within fighting range Rosepetal and Scarface pushed me towards Brutus and the whole gang ran off, leaving me to fight on my own. Brutus hit me, scratched me, bit me, punched me, and thrashed me. It wasn't so much a fight - more a reconstruction of the Massacre of Glencoe.

Every part of my body hurts - even my whiskers. But what's really puzzling me is why the gang suddenly took fright and ran away?!

11th October

Spent today lying on my favorite chair - too sore to move. I have aches in parts of my body I didn't even know existed. To add ignominy to injury the vet arrived unexpectedly and prodded me all over - making my agony even worse. How inconsiderate. I was too weak to fight back.

I overheard him saying to my humans, "He's okay."

Okay! I'm not okay! I'm in agony!!

12th October
(Anniversary of Christofurr Columbus discovering America.)

Snowball came to visit. She sat by my side for quite a while. She was most upset about my injuries and made me promise that all my cuts and bruises will be healed before the wedding. "I couldn't possibly marry someone who looks like a boxer that's just been pulverized," she said - jokingly, I think.

Although it isn't very warm, there was a little sunshine so I made the effort to go into the garden. I sat in my special spot under the sycamore tree. Almost immediately Brutus appeared at the fence.

"Been in a ballet dancing competition?" he asked sarcastically, "or are bruises the latest trend in feline haute couture?"

His insults continued but I was too weary to drag myself back indoors. "Why are you crying?" called a voice from above.

I told Bobin about my fight with Brutus and how he was teasing me. Bobin flew away. For the next few minutes there was a lot of chattering from the trees. Then a huge group of robins, sparrows and tits flew into Brutus's garden. They swooped and dived at him. Before he could get indoors he was pecked raw from head to tail.

"Don't annoy my friend again," said Bobin.

It's nice having friends.

13th October

10:30 AM: I am so stiff and achy that Brat-2 can cat-crawl faster than me. We played our chasing game. Sometimes he chased me - sometimes I chased him. He often bumped into my bottom causing me to do roly-polys across the floor. How we laughed!

5:10 PM: As I lay under the sycamore, Mucky squeezed through the hedge. "Is this my house?" he asked. He was lost! He had gone for an explore and couldn't find his way home. He had been wandering from house to house for hours. I took him back and warned him not to go far until he got to know the area better. Mr. 96 came running up the path crying, "Pusskins . . pusskins . . where have you been you naughty little kitty . . daddy missed you so." With tears running down his cheeks he picked Mucky up and gave him a big hug.

I am usually really good at assessing the character of humans. How could I possibly have thought he was a mass murderer?

14th October

Snowball came to see me. As it was raining, we went to the shed and lay on my worry blanket. It was very romantic, cuddled up together listening to the rain drops striking the roof.

We talked about our future together. We are so compatible. We both want exactly the same things. I want to be famous. She wants me to be famous. I want her to have everything she wants. She wants me to give her everything she wants.

"I could be perfectly happy just lying here with you forever," I whispered in her ear.

"Me too," she said affectionately, "if the shed was a castle and this filthy old blanket was a silk shawl embroidered with gold threads."

15th October

Woke up feeling fantastic. As I haven't seen Kitsune since my fight with Brutus I thought it was time I paid him a visit.

Kitsune was shocked to see all my cuts and bruises and wanted to know what had happened. Even though it embarrasses me to admit I'm part of a gang, I told him all about Killer and the Cosa Nostra and how we had attacked Brutus.

"So they made you, the smallest cat, go to the front!" he said.

"Yes," I replied hesitantly.

"And the two behind you pushed you towards the fierce dog!"

"Yes."

"And they all ran away!"

"Well . . . yes."

"And you say that these cats are your friends!"

"But Killer is a good friend," I said. "He insisted that I join his gang and he cured my fear of trees."

"Killer is no friend - he's an evil fiend," said Kitsune. "It's time he was taught a lesson."

"But he's to be best-cat at my wedding," I said.

"What! You must be mad!" said Kitsune.

I came home feeling quite miserable. I wish I could understand what's going on in my life.

16th October

Sat in the rain under the sycamore tree feeling despondent and wretched.

Bobin landed on my head.

"Why are you sad?" he asked.

"Because I'm confused about Killer."

"Why?"

"Because I don't know if he's my friend or my enemy," I replied.

"Why?"

"Because sometimes he's nice. But when I'm with him I usually get hurt."

"Why?"

"Because Killer makes it happen that way."

"Why?"

"I don't know," I said.

We sat in silence for a few minutes.

"Don't let Killer be your friend," said Bobin.

"Why?" I asked.

"Because I say so," he replied and flew away.

17th October

It was my turn to take Kitsune food today. It was with great trepidation that I made my way to the woods. I hoped he would be asleep so that I could leave the food and come away without having to talk about Killer. But Kitsune was awake and the first thing he said was "Has Killer been troubling you again?" Somehow I no longer felt the need to defend Killer and for the first time admitted the truth about him.

When I'd told Kitsune more of the nasty things that Killer has done, he said, "Lucky says there's a rumor going about that Killer chased Gypsy out of town. Is that true?"

I felt so guilty, I nearly choked on a furball. I confessed everything. When I'd finished I said, "I'm sorry I didn't tell you all of this before - but I felt so bad about being involved that I couldn't bring myself to tell you the truth.

"It's time I met Killer and his horrid friends," said Kitsune. "When is the next gang meeting?"

"At 8:00 PM on Sunday," I said. "In the alley behind the shops."

"You stay at home that night," said Kitsune. "I'll go in your place."

18th October

(On this day in 1963 French feline Felix, traveling on the Veronique rocket, became the first cat in space.)

4:00 PM: Wasps have built a nest in the wall at the far end of Lucky's garden. The noise of their constant fly-byes makes it impossible for us to sleep in the garden.

I told him to pack the entrance with mud. If the wasps can't get in they'll simply go and build a nest elsewhere.

We waited until there were no wasps about and Lucky scooped up pawfulls of mud and packed it into the entrance hole. He was just about finished when a young wasp came home.

"What are you doing?" she asked.

"That's none of your business," replied Lucky.

"Buzz off or we'll swat you," I threatened.

When we had completely blocked the entrance, Lucky and I went for a long walk, fully expecting the wasps to have moved nest by the time we got back. What a surprise we got - there were hundreds of wasps swarming around the nest.

"It was them," cried a small voice.

A group of rough, aggressive wasps flew at us. Lucky got stung six times. I got stung twice even though I hadn't blocked their nest.

"Fix our nest or we'll sting you to death," said a very large, antagonistic wasp.

Unfortunately we were grossly outnumbered and Lucky had to do what he was told.

The incident with the wasps proves that size really doesn't matter - provided there are hundreds of you and you are armed with deadly stings.

11:58 PM: I can't stop worrying about Kitsune - he's not yet at full strength and is no match for Killer and his gang. He'll be as badly out-numbered as Lucky and I were by the wasps. I hope he isn't hurt too badly.

19th October

7:00 PM: Spent today under my worry blanket. I'm a complete bag of nerves. I'm too worried to even eat. My tail is shaking so much, I look as if I'm swatting flies. If Kitsune gets killed I will never forgive myself for letting him fight my battles.

7:30 PM: In 30 minutes Kitsune will be killed.

7:40 PM: In 20 minutes Kitsune will be killed.

7:50 PM: I can't let Kitsune get killed on his own - I have to go and get killed with him.

20th October

10:20 AM: What a night that was!!!!

I ran to the shops as fast as I could. At 8:10 PM: I scaled the wall - the alley lay in front of me. The fight was in full swing. From my vantage point, I could see that Kitsune had already knocked out Satan. Facing him were Scarface, Rosepetal and Killer. Killer was lashing out with his sword-like claws, and Kitsune was ducking and diving to avoid being struck. Scarface was on Killer's left and Rosepetal on his right. They pushed forward forcing Kitsune to retreat. Suddenly I noticed Snapbone - he must have sneaked around behind the shops for he was about to spring a surprise attack from the rear. Snapbone leapt into the air. In a raging frenzy, I sprang down from the wall and just as Snapbone was about to land on Kitsune's back, I drove my claws into his chest. I sunk my teeth into his left ear and immediately tasted blood. We tumbled over and over on the ground clawing savagely at each other. He tried to break free from the grip I had on his ear but the more he struggled the tighter I bit. He jerked his head backwards - I heard a revolting tearing sound and Snapbone rolled away from me leaving a huge piece of ear in my mouth. He rolled a few more times then leapt to his feet. Hissing with anger and pain he leapt at me - with every intent of snapping my bones. Now, I do not have killer claws like Killer. They are not long or sharp like his. But when a cat leaps at full force onto them, they can do some serious damage. Snapbone's face discovered this the hard way. Crying with pain, he staggered away, blinded by the blood that was pouring down his head and into his eyes.

While I had been struggling with Snapbone, Kitsune had seen off Scarface and Rosepetal. Now there was only Killer to deal with.

"Not so brave without your gang," sneered Kitsune, as Killer backed himself into a corner beside the bins.

"Help me Adrian and I'll make you second in command," he begged.

"Get lost scumbag," I rasped.

Killer's back was now against the wall - he was trapped. "Meeeowwaaaarghhh," he cried and lunged forward, drawing his claws down Kitsune's face. Ignoring the blood gushing from his wounds, Kitsune struck Killer on the head, knocking him to the ground.

Killer was now on his back but, thrashing wildly with his razor sharp claws. Despite being slashed repeatedly, Kitsune lunged at him and sunk his teeth deep into his neck.

Killer fell silent as if dead. For a few moments he didn't move as Kitsune held him in his grip. Suddenly he found new strength from somewhere, struggled free, and attempted to escape by squeezing through Kitsune's legs. But Kitsune grabbed hold of his tail and swung him round and round like a shot putter swinging a putt. He let go. With a horrid crunch, Killer hit the wall and flopped to the ground. Kitsune struck him time and time again across his body and face.

"Stop," I cried. "You'll kill him."

Reluctantly Kitsune stopped. Killer lay flat out, barely conscious.

"If you ever trouble Adrian again," hissed Kitsune, "I will take great delight in killing you."

Killer lay motionless and said nothing.

"And you will never, ever run a gang again," said Kitsune. "Is that clear?"

"Yes," gasped Killer.

Covered in blood, Kitsune and I walked towards the pond to clean ourselves up.

"We did it Adrian," Kitsune suddenly yelled with delight. "We showed them!"

Every hair on my body tingles with pain but I'm so happy I don't care!!

1:07 PM: I was on my way to tell Lucky about the fight when I spotted Snowball hurrying across the park. When I called to her, she said, "I can't stop. I've just heard that Killer has been injured. I must go and be by his side."

Lucky was thrilled to hear all about the fight and made me tell him the story eight times. We went to the woods to celebrate with Kitsune and Lucky made him tell the story another six times.

11:53 PM: I have marked in my resolutions, 'I never, ever, ever need to be afraid of Killer, the evil cat who once ruled the Lane.'

21st October

11:58 AM: Snowball arrived at my door at 4:30 AM making very loud and aggressive meowing noises. I was forced to get Trousers out of bed so that I could go out to see her.

"What's wrong?" I asked.

"What's wrong!" she screeched rhetorically. "I'll tell you what's wrong!"

In the time I've known Snowball, I have seen her angry on more than a few occasions - but never like this. Her hair was standing on end. Her tail was as straight as an oak tree, and she thumped the ground with her paws as she spoke.

"You have ruined everything," she yelled.

Skirt came to the door to see what all the commotion was about.

"Don't shout so loudly," I beseeched. "Come on, let's talk in the shed."

"I got you into Killer's gang. I got you powerful friends," she yelled only marginally quieter than before. "You would soon have become important and able to get me the things I need. But you have thrown it all away by getting that stupid fox to beat up Killer."

"Killer was not my friend," I said quietly. "He took pleasure in causing me pain at every opportunity."

"That's just his way," she replied, yelling so loudly her spittle hit me on the face. "Are you not willing to take a little suffering for the sake of my happiness?"

"What's done is done," I said philosophically. "Let's not argue. Why don't we go for a long walk and talk about our future."

"No!" she said firmly. "Killer needs me. I must go and look after him. He's still in a lot of pain."

11:20 PM: This evening I played chase mouse with Brat and Brat-2. Brat swung the mouse-on-a-string, and Brat-2 and I tried to catch it. Brat-2 caught it twice, I caught it forty-three times and we bumped heads seven times.

22nd October

4:20 PM: I had just finished the sixth course of lunch and was about to take a nap in the shed, when Snowball came rushing into the garden. She was hyper-excited, hyper-ventilating and hyper-sexy.

"We must talk right now," she said.

We set off in the direction of the canal and Snowball talked eagerly as we walked.

"Killer has disbanded the gang," she said in a tone that suggested that this was something of national importance.

"Yes," I said, "so I heard."

"Don't you realize what that means," she said, in a near frenzy.

"I do," I replied calmly. "It means that I'm less likely to be caught stealing and thrown into Cattery-Prison and the cats of Bearsden will be able to spend their days sleeping peacefully without fear of intimidation."

"No! No! No!" she exclaimed irritably. "It means that you can take over as leader. It gives you the opportunity to become a cat of real importance.

When I said that I had absolutely no desire to become leader of a gang, Snowball became sulky. We walked slowly along the canal in complete silence. We reached the bridge and stood in the middle above the water.

"Do it for me," she implored, rubbing her body seductively against mine.

I looked down from the bridge and pensively watched an old milk carton floating slowly towards us. Snowball was right, this was a once in a lifetime opportunity. An opportunity for instant power and importance. But was that what I wanted? Below, the carton filled with water and sank to the bottom of the canal.

"I would do absolutely anything for you," I said slowly. "I would snatch a star out of the sky for you. I would even eat dog food if that would make you happy. But I will not become a gang leader."

There was a long uneasy silence, then Snowball said tersely, "Adrian, I love you - but unless you do what I tell you the wedding is off."

She slunk down the banking, through the nettles, and away from me.

Looking back momentarily she added, "You have until tomorrow to decide."

23rd October

(On this day in 1768 collars were invented by humans
in an attempt to enslave cats.)

6:00 AM: I lay awake all night struggling over what to do. I want to marry Snowball and be eternally happy but I do not want to be leader of a gang and be eternally on the run from the law. What a dilemma!! One minute I would resolve to become a gangster the next I would decide to be a law abiding but very unhappy cat. It's as difficult a choice as knowing what side of a door I want to be on. But I have now made up my mind.

7:00 AM: I went to Snowball's house and told her the wedding is off. She did not reply.

11:39 PM: Today has been one of the most miserable days of my life. I am unhappy, stressed, upset, discontent, frustrated, distraught and NOT engaged to be married to the most beautiful cat in the world. I seem to have two choices - starve myself to death or kill myself by overeating.

24th October

7:00 PM: In an attempt to cheer me up, Lucky took me to Windyhill Golf Course for a round of golf. The idea of this game is to stand close to the eighteenth hole and, when a ball lands on the green, try to get it into the little hole in as few kicks as possible.

If it takes four kicks this is called a Birdie, three kicks is an Eagle, two kicks is an Albatross and if you get it in with just one kick that is a Miracle.

I was in bad form as I was not really in the mood for playing and I let

Lucky win seventeen - one.

Later we went to the Nineteenth Hole Restaurant and raided the bins. There is always a delicious range of food scraps available there. It has a five star Bin-Club rating, so it's sometimes impossible to get a seat. I didn't really have an appetite and only ate the seven courses to please Lucky.

11:00 PM: My humans never complain about it, but really it must be such a disadvantage not having a tail. For goodness sake, even lowly creatures such as mice and dogs have tails. My humans show such bravery in spite of this woeful deprivation.

25th October

6:30 AM: I am taking positive action to change my lifestyle and find peace and tranquility. I have enrolled for a five day course at the Bud-Hist Centre. I start tomorrow - this is my very last day of stress.

11:20 PM: I have been feeling guilty about not visiting Old-Grey-Fur so I went to see her. We spent the whole day curled up on her couch, watching television and sleeping. I think that all she ever does is watch television and sleep. She really needs company - I must visit more frequently.

26th October

6:00 PM: Notes from today's Bud-Hist course:

Bud-Hism was established over two thousands years ago by a very wise cat called Bud. Bud was known as the Asleepened One, for he had attained immense wisdom by taking an abundance of naps. The Supreme Cat Bud reached such an advanced state of Enlightenment, that he was able to sleep twenty-eight hours a day and still have time for other important duties like napping and eating.

A key teaching of Bud, is to have no regrets about the past, not to brood over the future but to live in the present. This is summed up as, 'Don't mourn your past lives. Don't worry about your next life. Relax in the present and the future will be purrfect.'

Our main lesson for today was to learn the 'Seven Paths to Enlightenment:

The Seven Paths to Enlightenment
+ *Sleep*
+ *Nap*
+ *Slumber*
+ *Snooze*
+ *Doze*
+ *Siesta*
+ *Kip*

11:59 PM: I have been putting today's lesson into practice and can report that I feel a lot calmer.

27th October

Today we learnt about "The Four Feline Truths"

The First Feline Truth
Life can be frustrating and painful. The more ambitious a cat is the more frustrating and painful his life will be, for with ambition comes stress, disappointment and heartache. It is however, possible to minimize these unpleasant experiences by sleeping through each of your nine lives.

The Second Feline Truth

The origin of suffering is the attachment to transient things. Thus the desire for possession brings sadness rather than happiness.

By rejecting material possession such as velvet collars, plastic mice, and little-balls-with-dingily-bells-in-the-middle and by abstaining from pleasures such as catnip and excesses of cream, it is possible for a cat to reduce the amount of suffering in his life.

The Third Feline Truth

A cat can achieve a state of Nirvana, where his life is free from all worries, troubles, and complexity. This inner harmony is the realization that, provided you do absolutely nothing, others will do all the worrying, drudgery and hard work. This is the state that humans mistake for laziness and arrogance in enlightened cats.

The Forth Feline Truth

There is a path to the end of suffering - a gradual path of wisdom, virtue and laziness. The path should be traveled slowly with many naps and snacks along the way.

It was explained that an emotional balance can be developed by mindful meditation.

We tried a number of meditation techniques:

In the first we had to breathe in slowly and, while doing so, visualize a dove flying gracefully across a blue cloudless sky. As we breathed out we were to concentrate on its little wings flapping up and down. This didn't work for me, for every time I breathed out I saw a huge sparrow hawk swooping down and eating the poor little bird.

In the second exercise we were to imagine that we were in a peaceful place that we like. I couldn't stop thinking of being on Bluebell Hill with Snowball and the instructor had to send me out of the class because my crying was disturbing the other students.

28th October

(On this day in 1902 the Woolly-Blue-Thingy-With-a-Small-Tinkly-Bell was invented.)

Today we were given advice on how to live nine happy lives:

Ways To Ensure Nine Joyful Lives.
Be dignified – let dogs perform the tricks.
Sleep incessantly. It is the sole purpose of life.
Be prudent – never chase anything more than half your size.
Scratch wallpaper. It is one of the noblest pursuits.
Nurture patience – postpone all ambitions until your next life.
Chase string. It brings inner peace.
Be proud – you are a member of the family which includes lions,
tigers and cheetahs.
Climb curtains. It takes you to a higher spiritual level.
Be inquisitive – discover a thousand places to sleep.

I took the scenic route home, along the Lane. Killer was sitting there looking very poorly. As I walked past, he smiled and said nervously, "Hello Adrian, is it okay if I sit here?"

29th October

5:00 PM: Today at Bud-Hist class we were told that chanting a Mantra helps a cat focus on his inner self and reach a state of sleepiness.

At the start of each and every day I have to look into a mirror, hold my tail high, and recite the following mantra five times:

I'm a dynamic superhero,
I shall rid the world of mice,

I shall learn to fly like a bird,
I shall teach my human tricks,
I shall conquer vicious dogs.
But first I'll take my nap.

6:00 PM: Mucky came into the garden looking very pleased with himself. "I've just killed my very first bird all by my very own," he said proudly.

"Oh no," I cried, fearing the worst. "Was it a little robin?"
"What's a robin?" he asked.

I made him show me the feathers - thankfully it was just a rare and endangered osprey.

I explained what a robin looks like and made him promise never to kill one.

Because of my Bud-Hism training I'm now a vegetarian - I don't eat animals apart from mice, moles, birds, rats, turkey slices, voles, worms, spiders, butterflies, ants, flies and squirrels (if I ever manage to catch one).

30th October

7:00 AM: I recited my Mantra - unfortunately I couldn't take a nap afterwards as I needed to rush to the Bud-Hist centre.

7:00 PM: Sadly this was the last day of the course - I really enjoyed it and I'm now ready to start my new (Snowball free) life. I gave away all my possessions to Lucky (a three-quarters chewed plastic mouse, a pink-mouse-on-a-string, a red-plastic-ball-with-a-bell-inside, a purple feather and three catnip sweeties). I feel liberated, demotivated, calm (almost), and possessionless.

Today we heard the many Wisdoms of Bud. Here are a few of my favorites:

I purr therefore I am.

I sleep therefore I am happy.
I meow therefore I am fed.

From time to time engage in the seemingly trivial pursuit of frantically chasing a ball of wool. This frivolous activity will absorb all your negative energy and fill you with a wonderful sense of inner peace.

The five virtues that lead to a perfect existence are, selfishness, laziness, stubbornness, voracity and arrogance.

An enlightened cat acquires wisdom by spending long periods motionlessly staring into space considering issues of universal importance – such as contemplating the eternal question "Where shall I sleep next?"

Sleep gives structure to our lives providing something useful to do during the long periods between meals.

31st October
(Spooky Scary Day.)

9:00 AM: Folklore would have us believe that hundreds of years ago there were covens of cats that could do all sorts of evil magic. The story goes that, using their powerful spells, they could turn other cats into awful creatures like frogs and mice. It sounds unbelievable but apparently at that time thousands of cats were hung or drowned for allegedly practicing witchcraft. Even today there are supposed to be witches and wizards practicing evil magic. Spooky Scary Day is the time of year when their magic is supposed to be most powerful. What a load of nonsense!!

3:20 PM: I went to see Mungo and Gerry. I was shocked to find them in their garage mixing up a brew of snails, toadstools, mice tails and goodness knows what. I was about to run away, for to be honest at this point in my life I would rather not be turned into a frog, but I was spotted by Mungo.

"Hello Adrian," he said in a spine-chilling sort of way.

"Hi Addy," said Gerry in a sinister tone.

"I . . . I . . . I was just going," I stammered.

"You've only just got here," said Mungo menacingly.

"I've just remembered that I left the door open," I spluttered, giving the first dumb excuse that came into my head.

"Come," insisted Gerry menacingly, "have some of our lovely cocktail mix."

Cock tail mix! I really had no desire to be turned into the tail of a cock!

"Yes, have a drink," said Mungo trying to hypnotize me with his wizardly eyes.

"I don't think I'll bother," I said backing out of the garage.

"Suit yourself," said Gerry, disappointed that his evil plan hadn't worked.

As I turned to run I saw Mungo and Gerry drink the brew. They didn't turn into cock's tails. They didn't even turn into mice or frogs. They just smiled contentedly.

Their evil wizard strength must make them impervious to the magic powers of the cock tail drink.

1st November

11:57 AM: The Bud-Hism course has transformed my life. I feel at one with nature, in harmony with the universe. This morning, as I walked across the garden, and felt the earth beneath my feet I sensed a connection to a greater force, a force that unites all creatures in a bond of love with Mother Earth. I mentioned this to a slug that I accidentally trod on but sadly my weight had squashed her little life away.

4:20 PM: Spent the afternoon at Lucky's. Polly told us exciting pirate stories. Actually, I don't know why I ever disliked Polly - for a pirate parrot she's actually quite nice. I asked her when we could go treasure hunting but she said that the wind still isn't right.

8:05 PM: I have been very nice to my humans all day. I let Trousers sit on my favorite chair without attacking him. And I was not even the slightest bit condescending when Skirt took ages preparing my dinner.

9:45 PM: Trousers is still sitting on my chair - staring at the television with a comatose look on his face. I often wonder if humans are capable of intelligent thoughts while hypnotized by televisions or whether it causes their brains to stop working.

2nd November
(4000th Anniversary of the start of the Great Cat Dog Cold War.)

7:00 AM: While saying my morning mantra I was overcome by a great wave of sorrow. It came upon me like a thump on the head with a sadness mallet. I concentrated hard on the mantra but the more I did the sadder I became.

Suddenly I realize the cause of my distress - today should have been my wedding day!

10:00 AM: Brat-2 wants to play bumps but I need to be alone. I have come to the shed where there are no distractions and I can dedicate myself to being miserable.

My heart is broken and the happiness that was once inside has all oozed away like the blood from a decapitated mouse. How I miss Snowball. My life is pointless and empty without her.

11:40 AM: I have written a melancholy poem about my one and only true love.

Snowball

Snowball

Snowball

Snowball

Snowball

Snowball

Snowball

2:00 PM: Snowball - by now you and I should be married and I should be the happiest cat in the whole universe. Instead I'm the saddest cat in the shed.

11:42 PM: I have been thinking about all the things I miss about Snowball:

Her kindness.
Her gentleness.
Her generosity.
Her patience.
Her charm.
Her intelligence.
Her wit.

11:49 PM: It has just occurred to me - all the things I like about Snowball - she isn't any of them!

11:54 PM: It's Gypsy who is kind, gentle, generous, patient, charming, intelligent, and witty.

11:59 PM: I love Gypsy - not Snowball! It's her I'm pining for.

3rd November
(Saint Hubert of Liege Day - protector from dog bites.)

5:20 AM: I'm going to search the world for Gypsy. I will not rest until I've convinced her that I adore her and make her forgive me.

11:46 PM: Not knowing where I should begin, I used my natural male instincts. This told me to take the canal path to the City of Glasgow. Wow!! Glasgow is unimaginably immense. There are houses that stretch right up into the clouds. There are so many cars, crossing the road is a gamble with death. I walked until my paws were raw searching for my new true love. I saw many bedraggled, disheveled cats - but none of them were Gypsy. In desperation I stopped every cat in sight and asked if they'd seen her - but no one had.

I am desperately sad but my sadness is only making me even more determined to find my Gypsy. Yet I fear I never will.

4th November

6:00 AM: I barely slept last night. I spent hours trying to work out where Gypsy might have gone. She would surely want to be in a large town where food is plentiful. I decided to cross the Erskine Bridge and try Paisley. That's the sort of place a stray, who'd been kicked out of Bearsden, would go.

11:51 PM: Because my paws were aching, I tried a different tactic today. I went to the Abbey, which is in the town centre, climbed onto a tall tombstone and shouted "Gypsy, I love you," at the top of my voice. I shouted for over twelve hours with only a couple of breaks to dry off my fur when the Abbey caretaker threw buckets of water over me. Gypsy was definitely not in Paisley.

My throat is so sore, even thinking about eating is agony.

5th November
(Cat Scaring Night.)

6:20 PM: Another day of searching in vain. Today I searched all over Clydebank. I even tried the football ground, which was probably not one of my brighter ideas, for there was a game on. As I ran across the pitch, the ball hit me. It bounced twice then slid between the goalkeeper's legs and into the net. The referee blew the whistle ending the game. The fans went wild - I had scored the winning goal against arch rivals Yoker. The players adored me and wanted to adopt me as their lucky mascot - but I couldn't wait, even to be adored, I had more important things to do.

On the way home I met Lucky. As soon as I told him that I was looking for Gypsy, he insisted on helping. What a great friend he is. We'll set out again first thing in the morning.

8:00 PM: This is Cat Scaring Night - four hundred years ago a rebellious cat called Catesby, with the help of his human, Guy Fawkes, tried to blow up the Houses of Parliament in London. Humans have never forgiven Catesby for this, and every year they use fireworks to make frightening explosion noises and terrifying flashes in the sky. This is the night cats fear most. Even lying under the bed with my eyes tightly closed and my paws over my ears, I am shaking uncontrollably. I hope Gypsy is safe.

6th November

5:48 AM: Suffragette arrived with Lucky - they are both going to help. Suffragette insisted that we go to Loch Lomond. I doubt Gypsy will be there but, as I had no better suggestion, that's where we're going.

4:30 PM: We have arrived at Loch Lomond. After a snack we will split up and look in different places. Suffragette says that I have to look in the places we went when we came for the Cotton Thistle. This seems rather pointless - she would never go back there.

8:00 PM: I found Gypsy!! She was sitting forlornly on the lochside - at the very spot where we had talked all night.
I sat beside her.

"Fancy meeting you here," I said casually.

She did not reply.

"Nice weather for the time of year," I said resolutely.

No response.

"The loch is beautiful when it's misty and engulfed in rain."

Still no response.

"And doesn't the lightning make the mountains look so mysterious."

Resolutely she did not respond.

I wanted to say, "Gypsy, I adore you. I need you. I can't live without you. Please forgive me for being stupid, come home with me, marry me, and have my kittens." But somehow all that came out of my mouth was pointless drivel.

"Kitsune is missing you. Will you please come back and look after him?"

"Go away," she hissed. "You're upsetting me."

Dejected and deflated, I slunk away.

When I met up with Suffragette and Lucky I told them what had happened.

"Did you tell her that you love her?" asked Suffragette.

"Sort of," I replied.

"Boys are so stupid," said Suffragette. "Gypsy is here because she has happy memories of the time she was here with you. She obviously likes you a lot. But you've got a hell of a lot of groveling to do before she can forgive you."

11:00 PM: Feeling encouraged by Suffragette's kind words I am determined that tomorrow I will convince Gypsy of my love. Suffragette and Lucky have set out for home.

7th November

(Anniversary of Hertz Marconi discovering that he could receive radio signals through his whiskers.)

6:00 PM: Gypsy was walking aimlessly along the lochside when I caught up with her this morning.

"Can I walk with you?" I asked.

"It's a free world," she replied curtly, "at least for some cats."

We walked in silence for a while. I tried to formulate my thoughts into words that would tell her how I feel and convince her to forgive me.

"You look absolutely dreadful. You are terribly thin and your coat's as straggly as a sewer rat with diarrhea," I blurted out - immediately realizing that these were not the words I had planned to say. But she did look awful. Her coat is mottled and muddy and she's lost a lot of weight.

"Are you all right?" I asked.

"I'm as all right as a cat can be after she's been thrown out of town by someone she thought to be her one and only friend in the world."

Her words pierced my heart. I have caused her great suffering. I am not worthy of her love.

"Take care of yourself," I said, as I turned and walked away, "and do try to eat some food and groom yourself."

10:00 PM: I am not good enough for Gypsy. Tomorrow, I will return home and resign myself to spending my life as a lonely, miserably dejected (but intellectual) bachelor.

8th November

6:00 AM: During the night I had the strangest dream. I was in a dark cave with King Robert the Bruce. We had just lost a second battle against the English army and were in despair. As we sat forlorn in the cold dank cave we watched a tiny spider trying to spin a web. Twice the spider fell and twice it got up again full of determination. On the third attempt the spider succeeded in spinning its web and I was so moved by its perseverance, I jumped up and ate it.

"We have learned an important lesson," said, Bruce who was watching me. "If at first you don't succeed, have a good meal then try again." He gave all his soldiers a big bowl of porridge then went out and thrashed the English.

The dream made me think - perhaps if I tried giving Gypsy a good meal she would be more forgiving.

6:00 PM: I found a nearly fresh fish in the bins outside Brian's Fish and Chip Emporium in Luss Village and went along the loch in search of Gypsy. She was lying on the grass looking very weak.

"I've brought you a nice fish," I said.

"I have no use for food," she replied softly.

"You must eat." I insisted. "You're fading away to a Siamese."

"I have no reason to eat. No reason to live," she said.

"I want you to eat." I said. "I want you to live."

For a moment I thought she was about to smile but her eyes clouded and closed. I remembered Kitsune going into a coma and feared the same was about to happen to Gypsy.

"Wake up! Wake up!" I demanded.

With an effort Gypsy half opened her eyes.

"If you don't eat then I'll not eat and we'll both die."

There was a long silence and then she whispered, "Okay, I'll try a little."

We shared the fish - I made sure that Gypsy got the larger piece. We lay together for a long time. Gypsy slipped in and out of sleeps. When she slept I licked her fur clean - after twenty washes it began to look almost nice again.

In the afternoon I caught four voles and made Gypsy eat three of them.

After we had eaten, Gypsy was looking much stronger and agreed to walk along the water's edge with me. It was a bitterly cold evening and I did my best to shelter her from the chill wind blowing off the loch. The feel of her fur gently brushing against mine as we walked, gave me courage and I opened up my heart to her. I told her that she is the most wonderful girl in the world. I told her that I've split up with Snowball. I told her all about Kitsune fighting Killer and how Killer no longer has a gang. But most importantly, I told her I love her and on bended paws I asked her to marry me.

Throughout my long speech she had said nothing. When I proposed she looked deep into my eyes, as if searching my soul, finally she said, "I need to sleep. Let's talk about this in the morning."

8:00 PM: Above the loch we found a grassy knoll that is sheltered from the wind. Gypsy fell asleep immediately and I snuggled close to keep her warm.

Well - at least she didn't tell me to get lost.

9th November

6:00 AM: Gypsy has gone! She has run off in the night!!

7:00 AM: I searched the lochside but there's no sign of her - she's obviously made up her mind that she hates me.

8:00 AM: I was sitting by the water feeling miserable when I heard paw steps behind me. It was Gypsy.

"Where have you been?" I cried. "I thought you'd gone forever."

"Whenever I have a difficult decision to make," she replied. "I go for an early morning walk in the hills. The fresh, cool air helps me think clearly."

"So - will you marry me?" I asked eagerly.

"No," she replied calmly, with no sign of emotion.

"No?!" I shrieked, meaning, "You have broken my heart and soul into a million pieces. Without you my life is as pointless as a tin of dog food." "No!" she reiterated. "I will not marry you. But I will go back to Bearsden with you. It's too soon after what's happened to be thinking about marriage - let's give it time."

My heart leapt twenty meters.

We kissed.

I leapt twenty meters.

11:00 PM: After a good meal, courtesy of the bins at Brian's Fish and Chip Emporium, we set out for home. We talked and talked all the way. It was fabulous. Tonight we will sleep side by side on my worry blanket. I am so happy!!!!

10th November

8:00 PM: We held a reunion party for Gypsy in the woods with Kitsune, Lucky, and Suffragette. Four of the kittens managed to come too. Everyone is delighted that Gypsy is back. Rucky said that she wanted to be a stray when she grows up and Suffragette cuffed her across the ear. When the others had gone home, Kitsune, Gypsy and I had a long debate about living with humans.

Kitsune said that he could not possibly live with humans and argued that to do so would mean giving up his freedom.

I said that having humans to provide food and shelter gave me the freedom to do more important things - like sleep.

Gypsy said that because she likes traveling she is never in one place long enough to make it worth while training a human.

"What if you decided to settle down," I asked. "Would you be happy living with a human?"

"I might," she replied hesitantly. "But I'm not sure that I trust them." "They're not all bad," I said in their defense. "I can show you a few that are actually quite acceptable."

11:00 PM: We will spend tonight in the shed again - but really it's getting too cold for sleeping out. I do like to be warm and comfortable and would like to be snuggled up between my humans. I must persuade Gypsy to adopt a human before I freeze to death.

11th November

6:00 PM: There was a flurry of snow this morning. Gypsy didn't want to stay in the shed all day so we lay under the inadequate shelter of the rose bushes.

Bobin landed on the ground beside us.

"Why is white stuff falling?" he asked.

"Because the water in the atmosphere has frozen into flakes," I replied.

"Why?"

"Because it's very cold."

"Why?"

"Because it's winter."

"That's silly." he replied. "My mummy says it's little bits of cloud that have broken off," and flew away.

11:35 PM: I'm numb! I haven't warmed up all day. Winter in the shed is going to kill me. I'm a house cat for goodness sake.

12th November

In a desperate effort to heat up, I sneaked Gypsy into my house. We shared a bowl of Reconstituted-By-Product-of-Chicken-Including-Beaks-and-Feathers-in-an-Authentic-Hot-Tikka-Sauce, then settled down on my cozy, warm, comfortable, restful bed. We had only been asleep for seven or eight hours when Skirt came in.

"Aaaargh," she yelled. "There's a strange cat sleeping on the bed!"

Well what a cheek! Calling my new girlfriend strange! She may not be completely normal - but "strange" is taking things a bit too far.

Needless to say Trousers came storming in and, without even consulting me, grabbed Gypsy and threw her out the back door.

"I thought your humans were supposed to be nice," she said indignantly.

"I said they were nice," I replied. "I didn't say they were sane."

So my humans have really messed up! How can I persuade Gypsy to adopt a human after she's been treated with such disrespect?

13th November

Okay! So this page of my diary is extra, extra top secret - never to be read by anyone!!

Gypsy and I went on a mouse hunt this morning. It turned into a bit of a competition - though I don't think Gypsy realized.

I hadn't even started (I like to do some warm up exercises before mousing) and Gypsy had caught two mice. By the time one consented to being caught by me, Gypsy had caught five.

When the score reached Gypsy: 11 mice, 4 voles, 1 rat - Adrian 3 mice, 2 spiders, I suggested we do something different.

I have never been so humiliated in all my life - out moused by a girl!!!!

14th November

We woke this afternoon to the sound of Brat bursting into the shed to get his ball.

"Nice little pussy." he said, "You're a very cute cat."

I could see that Gypsy was pleased with this compliment and she was quite thrilled when Brat sat down beside her and stoked her gently. But la piece de resistance was when he took a packet of chocolate sweeties from his pocket and shared them with us. Gypsy was so happy she purred like a jet engine that has just been given a can of oil.

Later I said, "See, some humans can be nice and tomorrow I'm taking you to see a very special human friend." I hope Old-Grey-Fur likes Gypsy and doesn't throw her out!!!

15th November

Girls can be so sensitive!! I was going to take Gypsy to visit Old-Grey-Fur and wanted her to make a good impression, so I said casually, "Give yourself a good wash, I don't want you looking like a smelly old down and out." Well, you would have thought that I'd called her a poodle by the way she overreacted.

First of all she yelled that her fur was perfectly groomed and beautifully clean. She went on and on and on and on about this for thirty minutes.

Then she sulked for four hours and refused to speak to me.

Then she cried for an hour.

Then she said that her fur was such a mess that no amount of grooming could possibly fix it, and life wasn't worth living.

Then she spent two hours grooming and complained she had made it worse.

"Let me try," I said cautiously.

I spent ten minutes licking her fur into a fashionable style then spent three hours telling her that she looked terrific. Only then did she stop sulking and accept that she does not look like a tramp. By this time it was too late to go to see Old-Grey-Fur. We are at least speaking again - but only just. On reflection I'm glad I didn't tell her to be more like Snowball and take care of her appearance - I think that may have upset her even more.

16th November

(St. Gertrude's Day - patron saint of cats and protector from fleas.)

At last I managed to take Gypsy to inspect Old-Grey-Fur. Two meows at the door and we were in.

"Oh," said Old-Grey-Fur, "two cats today," which was stating the obvious really. But to be fair, she immediately took some freshly caught hamburger from the fridge and put it on a plate for us. I stood back and watched Gypsy eating. It was a delight. I suspect she has never eaten fresh hamburger before. She purred beautifully which pleased Old-Grey-Fur.

I took Gypsy for a tour of the house and showed her the most comfortable places for sleeping. She was thoroughly impressed but did complain that there was a strange smell.

"That, my dear," I replied indignantly, "is my musk - I have put a great deal of effort into spraying the place so it smells like this." What a cheek!

17th November

Good news - Gypsy has adopted Old-Grey-Fur. She followed my instructions and everything went like a dream. Here's what happened:

9:05 AM: Gypsy sat on Old-Grey-Fur's lawn meowing pitifully.

9:07 AM: Old-Grey-Fur peeped out of the window.

9:09 AM: Gypsy meowed louder and even more pitifully.

9:11 AM: Old-Grey-Fur opened the door to see what was wrong.

9:13 AM: Old-Grey-Fur brought out a saucer of milk.

9:13 ½ AM: Gypsy limped across the lawn and lapped up the milk as if it was her first nourishment in weeks.

9:15 AM: Gypsy rubbed herself around Old-Grey-Fur's legs - such contact tugs at a human's heartstrings.

9:16 AM: Old-Grey-Fur gently stroked Gypsy.

9:17 AM: Gypsy purred sweetly and stared straight into Old-Grey-Fur's eyes - breaking down any last resistance.

9:19 AM: Gypsy and Old-Grey-Fur adopted each other.

Humans are such a pushover!

18th November

Now that Gypsy is settled into her own house, I have moved back into mine. I love Gypsy a lot but I don't think love necessitates freezing to death.

Now that I'm warm again I can get back to having intellectual thoughts. Cold weather is bad for the brain - the colder it gets the lower your IQ becomes. I have decided to set up a society for gifted cats like myself. After much deliberation I'm calling it CATSA, which stands for Cats that are Smart Association. (I know this should really be CTASA but CATSA has a rather pleasant ring to it - and intelligent cats will understand my little play on words).

19th November

I have created a very difficult membership test for CATSA. I want to ensure that it's a society purely for the elite amongst cats. No one who gets more than one of the twenty questions wrong will be allowed to join.

Here are a few of the questions:

Q1) Which is the odd one out?
 a) A chair.
 b) A flea.
 c) Alaska.

Answer:: b) A flea - only a flea can bite.

Q2) How many eyes do four cats have?
  a) 2
  b) 4
  c) 6
  d) 8

Answer:: a) 2 - Obviously all cats have two eyes - if you don't count those that have lost one in a fight.

Q3) 6 kittens each have 6 fleas. Each flea bites 6 times per hour for 6 hours. How many bites is that in total?
  a) 1296
  b) None - flees don't bite, they suck.
  c) Far too many.

Answer:: c) Far too many

Q4) Which creature makes the nicest afternoon snack?
  a) An elephant.
  b) A mouse.
  c) A tyrannosaurus.

Answer:: c) A mouse - the other two are too difficult to catch.

Q5) Why do dogs bury bones?
  a) Because they think they are squirrels.
  b) Because they are stupid.
  c) To confuse archaeologists.

Answer:: b) Everything dogs do is because they are stupid.

20th November
(St. Murphy's Day of Travesty.)

6:45 AM: Today got off to a bad start. When the alarm rang, Trousers jumped out of bed. Unfortunately I was sleeping on top of him and landed with a thump on the ground. Trousers, selfish as ever, was so bothered about the tiny little bit of blood on his lacerated legs, he didn't even look to see if I was injured.

8:20 AM: When I leapt onto the table to get a closer look at the new flower vase, I accidentally slipped and knocked it over. It shattered on the ground spraying the room with little bits of glass. Fortunately, none hit me for I could easily have been killed. Trousers took a few direct hits and it took him some time to remove the shrapnel. From the fuss he made you would think that it was my fault.

11:50 AM: Went to visit Lucky. His door was lying open so I sneaked in. Lucky was surprised to see me - in fact he was so surprised he fell into a sink full of dishwasher. That will teach him to drink from the taps.

6:00 PM: After the drama of this morning I spent the rest of the day sleeping in the linen cupboard. As luck would have it, Trousers opened the door while I was in the middle of a scary dream. I got such a shock, the next thing I knew I was clinging on to his shirt for dear life. Fortunately I had recently sharpened my claws so hanging on was not a problem - though extracting claws from flesh can be difficult to do efficiently when the human is jumping up and down yelling. I eventually got back onto terra firma but not in the most elegant of ways.

11:52 PM: This has been a thoroughly unlucky day for me. Thank goodness it's almost over.

I'll just retrieve my yellow plastic ball from the stairs then get some sleep. Oooops - sounds like Trousers has got to the plastic ball before me.

21st November

10:00 AM: Tried the CATSA IQ test out on Gypsy and Lucky. They both got all the questions correct - either I have misjudged them completely or the test is too easy. But at least CATSA now has three members.

11:00 AM: While I was rewriting the test to make it much more difficult, Bobin landed on my head.

"Why are you doing?" he asked.

I told him about CATSA and the IQ test.

"Ask me! Ask me!" he begged.

Now it seemed a bit pointless asking a cute little baby bird questions that even a very intelligent cat would find difficult but, rather than disappoint him, I asked him the questions.

Much to my surprise he got them all right. Who would have thought he was an intellectual robin.

It's not possible for a bird to be a proper member of the exclusive CATSA as it's an elitist society for highly intelligent cats but I did make Bobin an honorary member. He flew off, all excited, to tell his mum.

4:10 PM: Put the new test to the test in the town centre. Not one cat failed! I'm pleased to say that the mouse that Mungo was carrying in his mouth got two questions wrong - of course being half comatose was a considerable disadvantage. The society now has four hundred and thirty two members plus one honorary member. (Had the mouse got one more question right I would have had to have made him an honorary member - posthumously.)

It looks like the town is full of exceptionally intelligent cats.

11:00 PM: Gypsy and I took a stroll along the canal. We met Snowball at the bridge. I introduced her to Gypsy and said that I hoped they could become friends.

"Friends with a cat of no fixed abode?" said Snowball, "There's nothing in the world that could please me more."

"Yes," agreed Gypsy. "I'd dearly love to be best friends with your ex-girlfriend."

"Gosh," exclaimed Snowball, looking Gypsy up and down, "you do look smart. Who does your fur?"

"Oh," said Gypsy, "I much prefer to do it myself."

"I thought as much," said Snowball. "It shows."

"And your fur looks so natural," said Gypsy with a grin. "At a distance it's almost hard to tell that it's dyed."

As Gypsy dragged me away, the girls stared back at each other over their shoulders and smiled - though for a moment I thought I heard hissing and spitting.

I'm so glad that they got on so well.

22nd November

Gypsy and I went for a walk up the Campsie Hills. She knows everything about nature. Rather than just call a bird a 'snack' like my friends do, she can tell that it's a Wagtail, Waxwing, Bullfinch, or whatever. She knows which plants are safe to eat and which will kill you or cause your tail to fall off.

We picked some suspicious looking toadstools and sat by a little burn to eat them. Even though Gypsy assured me six times that they were safe to eat, I was still rather worried. It gave me a rather difficult dilemma; should I let Gypsy eat the first one to see if she suffered a horrid painful death or should I take the first and sacrifice myself for her? I ate the first and didn't die.

Being with Gypsy is enjoyable in so many ways; she's clever and I like that in a girl, she's good fun to be with, and she doesn't put pressure on me to fight Killer, become powerful or to get her things. Admittedly, she's not as beautiful as Snowball but then Snowball could be an international model if it wasn't for travel sickness.

But I do find Gypsy very attractive! Attractiveness is a strange thing! It seems that you don't need to be beautiful to be attractive.

23rd November

Today we had the first meeting of CATSA. I was rather disappointed at the turnout. Only Gypsy, Snowball, Lucky, Gerry and Hamish turned up. Hamish has just recently moved to Bearsden. He's a Scottish Fold and comes from Stornoway on the Isle of Lewis. He's got a lovely accent - I can't understand a word he says.

I opened the meeting with a little speech thanking everyone for attending, then proposed that the topic of discussion should be, "Why are cats so superior to humans?"

I started the debate by stating, "Cats are so very, very superior because we spend most of our time in meditative thought whereas humans rush around doing millions of things that don't actually need doing."

After a few minutes silence, as everyone absorbed the intricacies of my statement, Snowball was the first to respond.

"Cats are superior," she said, brushing her fur as she spoke, "quite simply because we can wear sparkly collars."

"That's preposterous," said Gypsy. "Cats that don't wear collars are superior to humans and to collar wearing cats."

"Yeah, right!" sneered Snowball. "You're just jealous because you don't have a wardrobe full of designer collars."

"Stop...stop...stop," I interrupted. "Can we please keep to the point."

"In my opinion," said Gerry pensively, "there's nothing wrong with wearing collars but I do hate the ones with little silver bells. Personally I think I'm not such a good mouser when I'm wearing a silver bell. Now it may just be coincidence, but I have caught four-hundred-and-two mice when not wearing a bell but none when wearing one . . ."

"Hoots mon," interrupted Hamish. "Boys shudnae hae tae wear collars wae bells. Ra onny yins a boy shud wear are tartan yins."

"I hate collars," added Lucky, "ever since mine got caught on a branch when I was climbing a tree and I was almost hung."

I tried my very best to get the conversation back onto the topic of 'cat superiority' but without success and we talked about collars for over two hours. I did notice that Gypsy and Snowball had opposing views on everything and argued their points vehemently. Their passion and ferocity for debating, was the only highlight to the evening. At points their discussion got so heated that I thought they might come to blows. Who would have thought that collars could cause such an emotional debate?

24th November

6:00 AM: My humans and I had a major disagreement over the door. It all started at 3:00 AM when I needed to pee. As a favor to them, I asked to get out rather than do it on the duvet. What thanks did I get? None! Trousers complained terribly about getting out of bed. With all the fuss I just couldn't do a thing - I never seem to be able to pee when I'm upset. Outside it was cold enough to freeze the spinnerets off a silver plated arachnid, so of course I asked politely to get back in. How was I treated? With complete disrespect! I had to wait a full three minutes before the door was opened. Three minutes in the freezing cold would have killed a less hardy cat than myself. My humans really need to be taught a lesson in manners.

25th November

It was an accident and definitely all their fault! If they had learned their lesson from last night it would never have happened.

At 2:34 AM precisely, I discovered that I was absolutely desperate for a pee. I meowed courteously to let them know their door opening service was required - but no response. I licked Skirt's ears. I trod on Trousers' nose. But the only response was Trousers muttering some of his special words and Skirt saying, "Stop that - I'm not in the mood." (Though she may have been talking to Trousers).

I wish now that I hadn't drunk that sixth bowl of water before bedtime but as we say, "There's no point in crying over spilt milk - when you can lap it up."

Skirt and Trousers obviously don't know the saying, for they made a great point in crying over the spilt water I peed onto their duvet. I pointed out that it was their fault for not opening the door but despite that I spent the rest of the night shivering in the shed. It's so unjust.

26th November

11:00 AM: Trousers has been hammering, banging, and zzzzing at the back door for over an hour. He is working with a determination I have never seen in him before. As he hammers, bangs, and zzzzs, he has a mad look in his eyes. It's the same look that I often see when I tell a mouse that I'm not going to eat him and then say, 'only joking.'

11:58 AM: It's official - Trousers has gone insane. He has put a great big hole in the door and is staring at it like a kitten that has just unwound her first ball of wool.

2:12 PM: Well, pull my tail to wake me up! If I hadn't just seen it with my own eyes I wouldn't believe it. Trousers has fitted a cat-flap on the door!! What a nerve!!!

11:59 PM: I'm in such a bad mood! I'm so angry I have spent the day in the shed. Despite the freezing Artic like cold I will sleep here tonight. When I adopted and lovingly trained my humans I expected them to love me, serve me, and care for me. Opening and closing doors is a human duty. I'm sure it's written into the contract somewhere. My humans should consider it a privilege to open and close doors for me. It's one of the few things they're good at. And I hate these modern cat-flap contraptions - they are so impersonal.

27th November

1:00 PM: Skirt worked in the kitchen for most of the morning. She took a huge featherless bird out of the refrigerator and after some bizarre ceremonial ritual of covering it with butter and herbs (and stuffing stuff in a place that stuff should never be stuffed), she placed it into the oven. As it was obviously not a robin, I attempted to get my rightful share, but Skirt made it clear that she did not want the ritual to be interrupted.

6:00 PM: Lots of visitors, including Wrinkly-Skirt and Old-Grey-Fur came round to share the featherless bird. Gypsy came with Old-Grey-Fur. She said that the bird is a turkey and the very same as the slices that Old-Grey-Fur sometimes gives us. To be honest, I hadn't realized that sliced turkey was actually a bird - and certainly would never have guessed that it was a headless, featherless bird.

Gypsy and I sat in the dining room as all the guests sat around the table for dinner. Trousers carved the turkey and served it to each of the guests except Gypsy and I. I coughed a couple of times to let him know of his faux pas without embarrassing him but he just glared angrily at me. Fortunately, Old-Grey-Fur, was very generous and gave us lots of bits. Wrinkly-Skirt on the other hand was very mean, when I requested a slice from her she playfully stamped on my tail and otherwise ignored my request.

28th November

8:00 AM: As I ate my breakfast I felt a hundred eyes staring at me. I looked round and saw that the whole family were watching my every move. Impertinently they ignored my scowls. The moment I'd finished eating, Skirt said in a funny voice, "Come on Adrian, please try out your new cat-flap."

I gave her The-Stare to let her know that I will not use the cat-flap because:

> *a) It's freezing outside and I refuse to catch triple-pneumonia just for her amusement.*
>
> *b) I am not a dog that needs to perform tricks to gain her approval.*
>
> *c) I thoroughly resent that she wishes to relinquish her butler duties.*

"Addy out, Addy out," yelled Brat with an enthusiasm that irritated my nastier nature. While Skirt searched for the Elastoplasts, I found myself a warm place to rest.

Touché!! Point made!!

29th November

8:00 AM: We are at a standoff; my humans will not open the door for me and, despite all their encouragement, I will not use the cat-flap. Really it's Trousers' prize cactus that I feel sorry for - their pots are now full of pee and I know from experience that even big ones that have been lovingly nurtured for years, die quickly from over-peeing.

9:00 AM: I sneaked out while Brat had the door open, but I feel like a fugitive in my own home not being able to come and go as I wish.

9:20 PM: The wind, apparently, was blowing from the North-West this morning so Polly declared that this was the day we had to go treasure hunting.

After consulting the map for an eternity, Polly led us to the beach. "Shiver me timbers and blow ze cat down," she kept repeating, "the Pirates of Bearsden are gonna glitter with gold."

She made us run so fast I'd have had a heart attack if it were not for the thought of the treasures awaiting us. I imagined a huge chest so crammed with catnip that I could retire to a life of daily beach parties.

Lucky said that he hoped the treasure chest would be full of fresh cream. I pointed out that, since the chest had been buried for many years, any fresh cream might be nearing the end of its use-by-date. We reached the beach full of expectation.

"Arrrgh me mateys, ze treasure be due North-West of here," said Polly. It wasn't. Neither was it West, South-West, South, South-East, East, North-East, North, or even North-South. After hours of searching, Polly eventually admitted that she couldn't remember where she'd hidden the chest.

"Every time we come back to this point I notice something odd," said Lucky.

"What's that?" I asked wearily.

"We're sitting on a great big red X - just like the one on the map."

"Ze treasure, me buckos!" squawked Polly. "Now I remember where it's buried."

Sure enough, we were on a big red X that had been painted on the sand a long time ago. Eagerly we began digging - well to be more precise, eagerly Lucky and I began digging. Polly stood on my shoulder squawking encouraging comments such as, "Arrr, dig faster sea dogs or ye'll meet ze ropes' end."

It took over an hour to reach the Treasure Chest. It was not nearly as big as I'd imagined - in fact it was more of a Treasure Tin. My dream of daily catnip beach parties quickly downsized to annual parties.

Polly prized the lid off.

"Golden pieces of eight," she cackled.

"It's peanuts!" I gasped, "It's only peanuts!"

"These be precious peanuts you blaggard," she yelled. "Ze finest booty from Treasure Island."

"But what use are peanuts?" I asked.

"Arrrrr you useless scallywag," she squawked. "They be ze best tasting peanuts in ze world."

And to prove it, she ate half of them.

All that treasure hunting for a handful of peanuts. Never mind - it was good fun anyway, me hearties!

30th November

10:00 AM: Okay, so now I'm really insulted!!

Today Skirt got down on her hands and knees and pretended to be a cat. She cat-crawled across to the cat-flap and, while pushing it open with one hand, said slowly and loudly, "Out . . . o . u . t . . . o . u . t . . ." as if I was S . . T . . U . . P . . I . . D.

Brat-2 thought this was very amusing but I am deeply wounded. I was so disgusted I climbed out the window and went to see Gypsy.

6:00 PM: I sat for hours on the sofa while Gypsy rested on Old-Grey-Fur's lap.

"How are you settling in?" I asked.

"All right," Gypsy replied. "But humans take a lot of looking after."

She's right of course - especially ones like mine who do such stupid things as put cat-flaps on the door and pretend to be cats.

If Gypsy and I ever do get married, we'll have to decide whether to stay with our humans or become strays. That will not be an easy decision.

1st December

(3000 years since the invention of Vets.)

1:00 PM: Have just discovered that I have been left home alone. There is no food in my bowl. I have not eaten for almost an hour. I'm starving. I am like one of those neglected cats you hear about in the news. If the Prime Minister got to hear about this my humans would be put in prison. That would teach them!!

2:00 PM: I've searched the house from top to bottom - all there is for eating is a moldy old sausage that I found under a chair and Xin and Xout. What a dilemma - the sausage smells disgusting and eating the fish would mean getting my paws wet. Life is never easy!

3:00 PM: After eating the sausage, I jumped onto Brat's table and climbed on top of the fish bowl. I didn't expect glass to be slippy and the next thing I knew my head was under water and my bum sticking up in the air. In my panic to avoid drowning, I swallowed a huge mouthful of water and felt a scaly-fleshy thing slip down my throat. Fortunately I managed to haul myself free before I was seriously drowned. Everything was over so quickly, Xin didn't realize what had happened. As I sat beside the bowl, struggling to catch my breath, I heard him say, "Oh Cod-Almighty - Xout has been abducted by aliens!" I didn't bother to enlighten him.

9:00 PM: When Brat discovered that Xout (or Winky as he calls her) was gone he had a mammoth crying attack. Of course the usual inquisition followed. Skirt said that Tinky must have eaten her but Trousers (who blames me for everything) would have had me x-rayed if he could. Anyway what do they expect, I'm a cat, a natural hunter and fish are food after all!! Though to be honest I'm never comfortable eating anyone I'm on first name terms with.

2nd December

(3000 years since the invention of Vet Bills.)

Okay! Okay! So I've changed my mind. It's a cat's prerogative to do a bit of mind changing.

I used the cat-flap for the very first time and I must say that I take to new technology like a Persian to catnip.

It all happened thanks to Brutus (not that I'd thank him for anything he did). I was in the garden using my outdoor litter tray. While I was busy doing my business I heard the usual unfriendly insults from Brutus. At first I paid no attention for he's always tied up - but I quickly realized he was getting closer. In fact the brute was in my garden. I ran to the door and gave an emergency meow - but my uncompassionate humans didn't bother to hear me. By then Brutus had me trapped against the door.

"Use the cat-flap," came a sweet little voice in my head.

"Wow," I thought to myself. "I've got a guardian angel."

But then it dawned on me that it was Gypsy's voice.

"Quick," she pleaded from the hedge, "get inside."

Obediently I obeyed - I just closed my eyes, held my breath and pushed. Before I realized what I was doing I was on the other side of the door. Incredible! The cat-flap acts like a transportation device that takes you from one side of the door to the other! Amazing!! What a stunning piece of technology.

As I stood in the kitchen feeling very state-of-the-art I heard Brutus growl in amazement, "Where'd that bark-bark cat go?"

Now that I've entered the space-age I have decided to forgive my humans.

3rd December

10:00 AM: Lucky arrived at the door with an urgent message from Snowball. She says I must meet her at midday on Bluebell Hill. I wonder what's so important.

4:00 PM: When I got to Bluebell Hill, Snowball was waiting. She was perfectly groomed and wearing a designer collar. She looked stunning.

"Come, lie down beside me," she said gently.

Hesitantly I did.

"Remember all the wonderful times we've had lying here together," she said softly.

"Yes," I replied.

"We were so happy together. Weren't we?"

"Yes," I agreed.

"We were so much in love, the world could have started spinning like a wheel and we would not have noticed."

"Absolutely," I replied noncommittally.

"Isn't it so romantic lying here together again?"

I looked around. The hilltop offers a superb vista - the Sewage Works to our left, the Council Dump to the right and in the distance the silhouette of the Gasworks.

"Yes," I agreed, enthusiastically.

"Adrian," she said, tenderly looking me full in the eyes. "Are you ever sad that we split up?"

"Yes . . . I guess so," I replied, not quiet sure what to say - for to be honest recently my life's been so hectic I haven't really given Snowball a thought.

"That's good, she said with a smile, "for I have decided to forgive you and marry you after all."

Aaaaaaaaa," I spluttered incoherently.

"We'll get married next week. It's all arranged."

"I . . . I . . . need to think about it," I said, attempting to regain some control over my destiny.

"Think?" she yelled irritably, "Think!"

There was a few moments of embarrassed silence then she said more sweetly, "Of course you need time to think. This must have come as a surprise to you. I know you have resigned yourself to accepting second best with that stray, what's-her-name, but really Adrian, you deserve so much better than a smelly-flea-ridden-tabby-with-bedraggled-fur for your wife. You know we were made for each other. You go home and think. Then meet me tomorrow and I'll tell you all the arrangements for our wedding and honeymoon."

8:00 PM: I am so confused. I don't know what to do. A few weeks ago I loved Snowball more than anything in the world. Now I think I love Gypsy more than anything in the world. What if I'm wrong? What if I really do still love Snowball and only think I love Gypsy?

10:00 PM: To help me make up my mind I have created a list of the things I like and dislike about Snowball and Gypsy.

Snowball : Things I like.
She's beautiful.
She has great fashion sense.
She will help me become successful.

Snowball : Things I dislike.
She's a bully.
She's deceptive.
She's spiteful.
She's uncaring.
She's scheming.
She's manipulative.
She's vindictive.
She's inconsiderate.
She's selfish.
She's intolerant.
She's greedy.
She's domineering.

Gypsy : Things I like.
She's thoughtful.
She's kind.
She's attentive.
She's clever.
She's understanding.
She's gentle.
She makes me smile.
She's considerate.
She's sensitive.
She's witty.
She's caring.

Gypsy : Things I dislike.
Nothing really but I wish she would spend more
time grooming.

I am still completely confused. I am best at making decisions when there is only one choice.

4th December

4:20 AM: Couldn't sleep last night. I tried meditation but even that didn't help. I tried counting mice jumping over a mouse trap - but the snapping noise of metal against bone was counter productive.

I will go for a long walk and make my decision before seeing Snowball at midday.

5th December

11:00 PM: I am dying. This will be the last entry in my diary.

6th December

11:59 PM: I am not dead yet - but I'm so sore I easily could be.

7th December

I've had an accident. I was hit be a car on Thursday just after leaving the house. I must have been so exhausted I didn't notice it creeping up on me as I crossed the road. My humans have made me a special basket-bed beside the dining room heater and are making a great fuss over me. Gypsy hasn't left my side since it happened. She's taking such good care of me. Must sleep . . .

8th December

1:00 PM: I'm beginning to feel slightly less dead but my back legs feel as if they have no feeling. I can't move them at all. Although Gypsy puts a brave face on it, she has obviously been crying a lot. I hope there's nothing seriously wrong with me.

7:00 PM: During the times I'm awake, Gypsy keeps me amused with stories of her adventures and the amazing people she has met. She should really write a book about her experiences for other cats to enjoy. 'Down and Out in Paris and Glasgow' or 'Gypsy's Progress,' would be great titles.

11:30 PM: My legs are not improving and my humans are looking very worried. The vet shakes his head a lot when he visits - I know this is a bad sign. I fear that I may never walk again. Gypsy remains constantly cheerful but I can tell that she's worried too.

9th December

Despite my suffering, I wrote a thank you poem to Gypsy:

Gypsy
Patiently you sit by my side,
Fear and sorrow you try to hide,
Your compassion is beyond compare,
Revealing how much you care.

Gypsy, you give me hope,
And reason to fight for life,
So when at last I'm fit again,
Please, please, please become my wife.

I think I have some feeling back in my legs. It's an agonizing feeling of pain - but at least it's a feeling!

10th December

10:50 AM: My humans gathered round me this morning. Skirt placed a bowl of extra fresh cream a short distance from my basket.

"Come on Adrian," she said enthusiastically. "Come get some delicious creamy cream."

"Stupid creatures," I whispered to Gypsy. "Why don't they put it beside me?"

"I think they're trying to encourage you to walk."

"If I could walk I wouldn't be lying here like a stunned mouse," I said caustically.

"You must try Adrian," she pleaded. "Try for me."

Pulling myself up by my front legs I somehow managed to get onto all fours. I wobbled, but was able to prop my side against the basket to steady myself.

Gypsy purred loudly.

Skirt clapped.

Trousers cried at the vet's bill.

Brat yelled "Addy walk."

Brat-2 made raspberry noises.

"Keep going," said Gypsy. "You can do it."

I pulled myself forward. Awkwardly I took a few steps but the pain in my legs was unbearable and I collapsed onto the carpet.

Well done! Well done!" cried Gypsy through huge tears.

My humans were delighted too and wrapped me in a blanket so that I could rest on the carpet.

Well at least I have walked a few steps.

11:15 AM: I walked another few steps, ate the cream, then returned to my basket - maybe everything is going to be okay.

8:00 PM: Gypsy has been licking my back legs to help them heal - don't know if it will do any good but it sure feels good.

11th December

My humans tried the encouragement trick again - this time with salmon. Everyone, especially Gypsy, was delighted that I managed to walk without collapsing. After I'd eaten she said, "Ask me to marry you." I was so stunned I would have collapsed if I hadn't been lying down. "Will you please marry me?" I gasped.

"Let me think about it," she replied. "Ask me again tomorrow."

While Gypsy was away looking after Old-Grey-Fur, Brat and Brat-2 sat beside me. Brat showed me all the pictures in his dinosaur book and hit Brat-2 with it every time he tried to pull my tail. (I've never eaten a dinosaur - I wonder if they taste like mice.)

The pain has almost gone from my legs.

12th December

4:00 AM: "Will you marry me and make me the happiest cat in the universe?" I asked, the moment I awoke.

"Yes," replied Gypsy dreamily, and fell asleep again.

I do hope she remembers accepting my proposal.

11:50 AM: Against Gypsy's advice we are going to visit Lucky and Suffragette. Even though it will be a long, strenuous walk, I desperately want to tell them about the wedding.

4:00 PM: On the way to Lucky's we met Snowball. She held her head high as she hurried past and ignored us completely. I didn't bother telling her that Gypsy and I are engaged. Before we could tell Lucky and Suffragette, they announced that they are getting married. What a surprise! I would never have expected that! We have decided to have a double wedding on the 20th of December.

8:40 PM: The humans have bought another fish to replace the one I ate. Brat has named it Winky-2. How very unimaginative. She does look delicious.

13th December

Skirt used the same encouragement trick on Brat-2 that she used on me - except it was with a biscuit rather than cream. In the same wobbly way that I walked, Brat-2 took a few steps in an upright position before collapsing onto his bottom. Skirt was delighted but I feel that this is a backward step in humankind's evolution. After all he did master cat-crawl without any encouragement tricks.

14th December

My humans have given me the best-present-ever - a bird-catching-table. They have loaded it with seed and placed it in the garden for me. Already there are more birds in the garden than I've ever seen at one time. Over the cold winter months, when mice are scarce, this will provide me with some lovely tasty snacks. I must warn Bobin to whistle when he's on the table so that I don't eat him.

15th December

Devastating news - Kitsune is leaving Bearsden tomorrow. He says he doesn't want to live in a town full of cars and people and is going to the Campsie Hills where he hopes to find his parents.
I feel quite miserable - I shall miss him such a lot.

16th December

(Boston Catnip Party - In this day in 1773 American cats protest against British taxes on catnip.)

Lucky, Suffragette, Gypsy, all the kittens and I gathered at the woods to say goodbye to Kitsune. It was a very emotional occasion with lots of tears. I managed not to cry but only by biting hard on my tail.

Brat-2 said his first human word today. Skirt thought it was 'mummy,' Trousers thought it was 'daddy,' but I know it was 'Addy.'

17th December

11:45 AM: Brat-2 is a health hazard! Now that he walks on two legs there is the constant danger of him collapsing on top of me. From the way he giggles, when he lands on my tail, you would almost believe that he's doing it on purpose.

6:00 PM: My humans have given me the best-present-ever. This is the second best-present-ever they have given me this week. They have planted a tree in the living-room. Now I can practice climbing without the inconvenience of going out in the cold. My humans think of everything!

10:00 PM: It's amazing beyond belief! They have covered my tree in a kaleidoscope of tinsel and put dangly little bobbles all over it for me. There is even a set of tiny lights so I can climb in the dark. Unfortunately they're not working very well - they glow for a second, then they don't, then they do, then they don't.

I managed to get a gold bobble off the tree by giving it a good hard whack. I had brilliant fun chasing it around the room. My humans found this very amusing - especially Brat and Brat-2 who joined in the chase game. I was best at bobble chasing and even managed to smash it into hundreds of pieces.

11:00 PM: Tonight I will sleep under the tree - there is a wonderful smell of pine just like in the woods. I hope Kitsune is safe and has found his parents.

18th December

We had a CATSA meeting in the park. Ten cats attended including Lucky, Suffragette, Gypsy, Mungo, Gerry, Rucky and Yucky. Two new cats attended; Fling - a small ginger cat who said absolutely nothing during the meeting, and a grey Manx named Morris who interrupted every two minutes by saying, "That's so profound."

Today's topic was, "Were cats better off three thousand years ago when the Egyptians revered us as Gods?"

Suffragette made the point that although we are not now considered Gods, little has changed and humans still think we are adorable.

"Although humans adore us they no longer build temples to worship us," said Lucky. "And I think that that is for the better."

"That's so profound," said Morris.

"Not all humans adore us," said Gypsy. "In fact some treat us ever so cruelly."

"That's so profound," said Morris.

"Well I would like to be treated like a God," I said. "But I draw the line at being mummified before I have completed all my nine lives."

"That's so profound," said Morris.

Little Rucky cleared her throat and said, "Catkind is very special; supreme amongst all animals. And even though we are no longer revered as Gods, the whole of humankind still worship at our paws. Yet we are neither conceited nor vain. Despite their adulation we are unaffected and remain, in all ways, perfect."

"That's so profound," everyone said.

By now it was snowing heavily so we abandoned the philosophical discussion in favor of sliding down the snow covered hill on our bottoms.

19th December

10:25 AM: Trousers and Skirt have put trillions of brightly wrapped presents under the tree. I think all their kindness is to celebrate my not dying. They don't want me to open the presents yet for, when I claw at the wrapping, they make a loud, "sssssshhhhhhhhhhhhwwwing" noise.

I suppose I should show my appreciation by giving them something in return for all these gifts.

2:10 PM: I went to the canal and caught the biggest rat in the universe. What a brute! He didn't want to be caught and tried to catch me instead. Dragging him all the way home was a real marathon but the look on my humans' faces when they see this magnificent present will make it worth all the effort.

Getting him through the cat-flap proved a bit tricky for it snapped shut on the rat and won't open again - the creature is stuck in the twilight zone between in and out. I'll have a short nap then I'll have another go.

6:11 PM: What an ungrateful lot! No 'thank you'. No 'well done'. No 'what a nice rat.' Just a great deal of fuss.

I had not been asleep for more than two hours when I heard Skirt scream like she'd been caught in a mouse trap. After a while I felt obliged to go and see if I could help her - but by then she'd phoned Trousers at the office and made him come home. I got into the kitchen just as he prized the rat out of the cat-flap.

"I suppose we have you to thank for this," he said.

I smiled and purred gently, swelling with pride.

"Well it just won't do!!" he hollered, glaring at me.

"Won't do?" I thought. "That's about the biggest rat in all of Scotland - what do you expect?"

With tears flooding from his eyes, Brat gently patted the dead rat.

"Poor little bunny," he said.

"Bunny? ... Ooops! ... Now I've had a proper look, it does have rather long ears. Oh well my mistake ... never mind - these things happen"

But my humans did mind - big style! In fact they minded so much they buried the bunny with full military honors. Trousers wrapped him in cotton wool and placed him in a box. Then we had a funeral service in the back garden. As the little creature was laid in its final resting place, I sang, "Will ye no come back again." But my humans didn't really appreciate the irony. Humans have no sense of humor.

Nobody is speaking to me but I don't care - tomorrow I marry the ~~most beautiful~~ most wonderful cat in the whole world.

20th December

8:00 AM: Today is the big day. My wedding day. This is the most important, wonderful, amazing, exciting day in all of my nine lives. I'm terrified!

9:20 AM:　　In just a few minutes I will lose my freedom forever. Was this such a good idea?

11:30 PM:　　Yippee!! I'm Married!!! It's brilliant!!!!

Here's what happened on my extra special day:

9:40 AM:　　When Lucky and I reached Blueberry Hill every cat in town was there - except Snowball and Killer of course. What a surprise to see so many guests - we had only invited our closest friends.

Polly was flying overhead squawking, "Ahoy me mateys, come see Adrian and Lucky dance ze Hempen Jig. See them walk ze gangplank of matrimony. Watch them drown in a sea of stormy married bliss. Yo ho ho - then we'll splice ze mainbrace with bottles of Nelson's Folly and party till we all heave-to." With a "shiver me timbers," she settled on the branch of a tree beside Bobin.

9:44 AM:　　Kitsune and his parents arrived. I was surprised and delighted to see him and thrilled that he'd found his parents.

"It's great to see you," I said, rubbing my head against his.

"When I heard that my best friends were being wed, wild dogs couldn't have kept me away," he replied.

Kitsune's parents seemed nice and when they realized that some of the guests were rather nervous around foxes they offered to sit at the very back.

9:52 AM:　　Pious arrived. Pious is the cat that lives in the church. He's a bit dottery, but Suffragette had asked him to lead the ceremony. He asked me who was being buried. When I told him it was a wedding he said, "Pity, I prefer funerals. They're so much cheerier." It took me ages to explain that Lucky and I were getting married but not to each other.

9:57 AM:　　Gypsy and Suffragette had still not arrived.

10:03 AM:　　No sign of our brides-to-be. I was beginning to get worried that they had changed their minds.

10:11 AM:　　Still no sign of Gypsy or Suffragette.

Bobin began chirping, "Why are we waiting...why are we waiting..."

Polly joined in with a chorus of, "Hey ho, the girls have run ze rig -

Adrian and Lucky have been keel hauled. Ho ho ho."

10:22 AM: At last Gypsy and Suffragette arrived - I had been getting very concerned and embarrassed!!

10:23 AM: Gypsy and Suffragette walked down the aisle towards us. Behind them came the six page-kittens. They looked angelic - all except Hucky, who kept tripping up her brothers and sisters.

10:25 AM: Gypsy stood by my side and we smiled. She looked stunning - I noticed she was wearing a beautiful collar made from white satin and covered in a rainbow of jewels.

"Where did you get the pretty collar?" I whispered.

"It was lying on the doorstep this morning."

"Did Old-Grey-Fur get it for you?"

"No she was as surprised as I was when we found it."

10:28 AM: Pious started the ceremony; fortunately remembering it was a wedding. He said a few words on the importance of marriage and the need for love then went on at great length about how difficult it is for an old cat to keep a church free from mice all by himself. Quite a few of our guests took the opportunity to have a nap.

10:46 AM: We exchanged vows. Pious declared that we were officially married. Gypsy and I kissed. Suffragette and Lucky kissed. Then we all hugged.

10:48 AM: The wild party began - we had an amazing celebration!!

21st December

11:00 AM: Lucky, Suffragette, Gypsy and I are honeymooning at Loch Lomond. We are staying in a barn that belongs to a friend, Bonnie-Banks. We are sharing the barn with a herd of cows, so it is unbearably noisy, incredibly smelly, but otherwise perfect. Bonnie-Banks has gone to a lot of trouble preparing two special sleeping areas in the loft section above the cows. There is something very primordial about sleeping on hay - it makes you feel at one with nature. Not as natural as a warm bed with silk pillows of course.

11:22 PM: It was a cold, windy day and we were content to just laze around in the barn. Bonnie-Banks caught all the food - it was an experience watching him catch mice. Somehow he could sense exactly what route a mouse would take - even before the mouse had thought about leaving its nest! Whenever a mouse popped its head out of a burrow, the first and last thing it saw was Bonnie-Banks. Professional mousers are so much better than we amateurs. I asked him if he enjoyed mousing. He said that there's not the same job satisfaction there was in the good old days but at least the hours are good.

In the evening we sat on Luss Pier and watched the moonbeams dance on the water. It was so romantic. Lucky summed up our feelings when he said, "I couldn't be happier if I won a million mice in the national lottery."

What an idyllic day - married life is wonderful. Gypsy is the perfect wife.

22nd December

Bonnie-Banks took us to another barn to get milk. The moment we entered, I noticed that the farmer was squeezing a cow's udder causing a white liquid to squirt into a bucket.

"What's that?" I asked.

"Milk," replied Bonnie-Banks. "The farmer is milking the cow."

"Yuck," I said. "How disgusting." I didn't realize that milk was squeezed out of a cow's private parts - I'll never drink the stuff again!

Bonnie-Banks took us on a tour of the farm; and showed us the sheep, pigs and chickens. I thought cows were smelly but you would need to spray the pigs for a year to remove their pong. Chickens are the funniest creatures I've ever seen. Whenever we got close to them they clucked, "Help! Murder! Help! Murder! Crazy Killers! Crazy Killers! Help! Murder! . . . " and other stupid things.

Silly really - for part of Bonnie-Banks' job is to make sure that they are safe.

Later we went on a haggis hunt on Ben Lomond. Unfortunately haggis move very quick and only Bonnie-Banks managed to spot any. He explained that haggis have two short legs on one side of their bodies and two long legs on the other side so that they can run round the mountains. He caught one to show us but it looked to me as like a rabbit with bits of its legs bitten off

After the haggis hunt we set off for home. It was a short honeymoon but a lot of fun.

23rd December

Brat-2's upright walking has entered a new phase - walk and throw. Wooden blocks are his favorite. Televisions, radios, ornaments and my body are his targets. I shall keep well out of his way until he reaches a less dangerous phase.

24th December

Gypsy came through the cat-flap to visit and was quickly ejected by Skirt. My humans are so inconsistent, intolerant and infuriating! Married life will need to take place at Gypsy's house and the shed. Oh well - at least I have a place to go when I want to be alone.

25th December
(Day of Receiving Nice Things.)

8:00 AM: This morning was organized mayhem. My humans were up at 5:00 am. This is especially unusual for Brat for he hates getting up even more than he hates going to bed.

For hours everyone tore the wrapping off parcels until the room was tail high in colorful, crinkly paper. I got a yellow ball, a catnip-chocolate-mouse, a woolly rabbit (I sense a bit of sarcasm), a green collar (which I hid under the bed), a multicolored-feather-thing-with-a-string-attached, and enough boxes to last nine lifetimes.

What a morning - I must take a nap.

5:00 PM: Gypsy and I had two massive dinners. First we ate with Old-Grey-Fur - she had made a huge meal for her visitors and insisted that we got more than our fair share. (It makes me sad watching humans eat. They are incapable of bending down to lap up their food and need to resort to using knives and forks.)

We were going for a post massive-dinner walk, when I heard Skirt shouting, "Adrian, din-dins." Much to my surprise, she didn't mind when I brought Gypsy in. (Humans are unpredictable - one minute it's okay for me to have guests, the next minute they're getting all uppity about it.)

Gypsy and I sat by the table as my humans ate. To my astonishment they all gave us bits of their food - even Trousers and Wrinkly-Skirt. My humans never cease to amaze me!

10:20 PM: It's been a very special day - but I've eaten so much I could sleep for a week.

26th December

(Box-In Day - A time for catkind to celebration the mystery of the box.)

10:20 AM: I was abducted by aliens! I had just awoken from a lovely dream, in which mice were all made of fresh cream, when I heard a strange whirring noise. A silver flying-saucer flew down from on top of the refrigerator and landed next to my basket.

Two, four-tailed purple aliens descended a little stair. Their big antenna eyes fixed me in a hypnotic stare. One raised a red stun gun and blasted me on the head. Everything went fuzzy for the next few hours. I have a vague recollection of being taken onboard their spaceship and thoroughly examined. Unseen voices talked about me;

"This is a very fine creature."

"Yes he is intelligent, strong and healthy."

"Not what we expected."

"If he is typical of the life form on Earth we dare not attack."

"No - we must search for a planet inhabited by weaker, less intellectual creatures."

"Our mission here is ended. We must go."

The next thing I remember is sitting in my basket with an aching head, feeling all woozy. Brat and Skirt were staring at me in a strange way. Everything was hazy but I'm sure Brat was holding a toy that looked just like the spaceship. Skirt was scolding him and telling him to be more careful where he threw things. Brat giggled.

6:00 PM: Spent ages investigating all the boxes I received yesterday. One of the biggest mysteries of boxes is that they quickly disappear. Already half of mine have gone. I wonder if there is a connection with the Flying-Saucer that I saw this morning?

11:48 PM: I have eaten a ton of leftover turkey today - before long I'm going to need a bigger cat-flap.

27th December
(Overindulgence Recovery Day.)

10:20 PM: Caught a big fat mouse this morning. He must have overdone the cheese during the last few days for he could barely run. I toyed with him a bit but I just didn't have the appetite to eat him. I hope I'm not coming down with Not-Able-to-Eat-Sickness. Gypsy feels the same so we slept in the shed all day.

28th December

As I was walking along the Lane, I was confronted by Killer.

"Have you lost something?" he asked.

"No," I replied, puzzled.

"What about your tail?" he said.

I looked round to check.

"My tail is where it always is."

"If you're still in my Lane in two seconds," he hissed, "It will be hanging in my trophy room."

"There's no need to take that attitude," I said.

"Now that your filthy fox friend has gone I can take any attitude I want."

To prove the point he scratched me right across my forehead. I made a hasty retreat.

"I'm going to make your life a misery," he called after me.

I told Gypsy that I'd cut myself on a rose bush - I don't want her worrying.

29th December

6:00 PM: Gypsy and I had our first real argument since we married. It all started when I said that my multicolored-feather-thing-with-a-string-attached was nicer than the one Old-Grey-Fur gave her. She said that hers was much nicer and before long we were at complete loggerheads.

I'm afraid I got rather hot tempered for I felt it necessary for Gypsy to realize that my multicolored-feather-thing-with-a-string-attached is by far the better. Gypsy argues by not speaking. This is so frustrating for, if she doesn't speak to me, how can she hear what I need to say.

11:45 PM: We have kissed and made up. But we almost had our second argument when I said that her multicolored-feather-thing-with-a-string-attached was nicer than mine and she insisted than mine was by far the nicer of the two.

30th December

10:05 AM: Snowball was sitting under the rose bush when I went out for my morning constitutional.

"Let's go for a romantic walk," she said, brushing up against me.

"I'm a married cat!" I replied.

"That makes you even more desirable," she said, beaming me a big sexy smile.

I was stunned into silence - but I must admit I felt flattered.

"You should never have married that what's-her-name, I'm much more beautiful."

"Please go away," I pleaded, desperately. "Gypsy will be here soon."

"Okay," she replied. "But I'll be back - I always get what I want."

7:00 PM: Gypsy and I had a long discussion about our future. We both have nice houses and acceptable humans; it would seem a shame to give everything up to become strays.

"And anyway," said Gypsy coyly, "it will soon be spring - perhaps we should be thinking of starting a family."

"That would be nice," I said, "I'd like six boys."

"Well I'd prefer six girls," said Gypsy.

"How about six boys and six girls?"

And so it was agreed.

11:00 PM: I tried to tell Skirt that I'm not leaving and will soon be starting a family, but she seemed to think I wanted my tummy tickled. This misunderstanding continued for three hours.

31st December

What a brilliant year this has been! I've fallen in love for the first time and fallen out of love for the first time. I've married the best girl in the world. I've added a new human to my family. I've made friends with a robin, a fox and a pirate parrot. I've been the enemy of an evil gang leader, best friends with him and then his enemy again.

My one regret is that there just hasn't been enough time for sleeping.

Next year I am determined to become wiser, braver, and humbler. By the end of the year I will be idolized by everyone.

MY NEW - NEW YEAR RESOLUTIONS

1) *I will not be condescending to my humans.*
2) *I will not maul the vet.*
3) *I will only give my best friend Lucky really, really good advice.*
4) *I will not be afraid of Killer – the evil cat who rules the Lane.*
5) *I will be decisive – particularly about being in or out.*
6) *I will become the World's most famous cat.*
7) *I will not get fleas.*
8) *Most importantly: I will promote World Peace between Cats, Dogs and Mice.*